CN00693591

BROKEN MIND

BROKEN REBEL BROTHERHOOD: NEXT GENERATION

ANDI RHODES

BLUE JOURNEY PUBLISHING

Copyright © 2021 by Andi Rhodes

All rights reserved.

No part of this book may be reproduced in any form or by any electronic or mechanical means, including information storage and retrieval systems, without written permission from the author, except for the use of brief quotations in a book review.

Cover Artwork - © Amanda Walker PA & Design Services

For anyone who has ever been afraid to speak up. You are not alone and you deserve to be heard.

ALSO BY ANDI RHODES

Broken Rebel Brotherhood

Broken Souls

Broken Innocence

Broken Boundaries

Broken Rebel Brotherhood: Complete Series Box set

Broken Rebel Brotherhood: Next Generation

Broken Hearts

Broken Wings

Broken Mind

Bastards and Badges

Stark Revenge

Slade's Fall

Jett's Guard

Soulless Kings MC

Fender

Joker

Piston

Greaser

Riker

Trainwreck

Squirrel

Gibson

Satan's Legacy MC

Snow's Angel

Toga's Demons

Magic's Torment

BROKEN REBEL BROTHERHOOD

THE ORIGINALS

A NOTE FROM ANDI

Broken Mind was not an easy story for me to tell. All of my books deal with difficult topics but for some reason, Ruby and Liam's story cut deep. I cried, laughed, and bled along with them at every turn and I hope you'll do the same.

Broken Mind addresses some very real, and potentially triggering, issues that women in the military, and in general, face on a regular basis; however, Broken Mind is a work of fiction and is not based on any real person or event. Broken Mind is not a representation of my thoughts and feelings about military procedure or policy. I am an immensely proud wife of a US Navy veteran and the words on the following pages are the result of my creative mind and should be read as such.

That being said, sexual assault does not discriminate. There is evil in the world and sometimes that evil is masked by power, prestige, money, title, etc. No person should ever be made to feel that they cannot speak up about what they are experiencing, nor should they feel like they don't deserve justice.

If you or someone you know is the victim of sexual

assault, I urge you to contact the National Sexual Assault Hotline at 1-800-656-4673 and military personnel can contact the Safe Helpline at 877-995-5247 or visit www.safehelpline.org.

Now, sit back and enjoy Ruby and Liam's journey in Broken Mind! Oh, and grab a box of tissues, maybe a glass of wine or shot of Tequila... you're going to need it!

His love roared louder than her demons.
-Anonymous

PROLOGUE

RUBY

Five years ago...

"No one will believe you, Private."

Sergeant Jensen stands in front of the door, arms crossed over his chest and his uniform as neat as always. I keep my eyes averted as I pull my pants back up, not bothering with my panties. I shove those in my pocket and turn in circles to try and locate my Army-issued uniform shirt.

"Maybe." I shrug. "Maybe not. But I'll do everything I can—"

He shoves away from the door and stalks toward me. I'm not fast enough to stop him from wrapping his fingers around my throat and pushing me against the wall. His elbow grazes my bra-covered nipple, and a glint enters his eyes.

"They won't believe you," he snarls. "Because there's

nothing to believe." He squeezes, cutting off my air supply. "You got that?"

I open my mouth to respond but nothing comes out, so I nod instead.

"You better remember your place, Private. The Army doesn't like it when their Sergeants are falsely accused of sexual misconduct."

Call it what it is you piece of shit. Rape. It's rape.

"Besides, from what I hear, your behavior has been erratic lately. I'd hate for your *mental instability* to become a permanent part of your military record."

The threat is clear: report his actions and I'm labeled a crazy woman who can't hack it in the military.

Jensen releases me and I slide down the wall. He glares down at me and I have to force myself not to shrink away from him. I want to but then he wins. More than he already has.

I tried to report the first time but that went nowhere. Sure, it earned him an interrogation, but in the end, there were no consequences. Except to me. The second time was more brutal and that's when the threats started. For the last two years, I've endured Jensen's attacks and I've kept my mouth shut.

"See you next month."

Like clockwork.

With that warning, he turns on his heel and leaves. He doesn't close the door behind him. He never does. It's like some sort of sick game for him to see if I can get to it and pull it shut before anyone sees me.

I scramble to my feet and do just that. Once I engage the lock, I allow myself to breathe. I suck in air so fast that spots dance in my vision and I sway on my feet. I brace my hand on the wall to steady myself.

I see the camouflage of my uniform shirt peeking from

beneath one of the tables and I bend down to pick it up. I stare at the name tag and tears spring to my eyes.

All I've ever wanted is to be in the Army. To follow in my father and uncle's footsteps and serve my country. My mother begged me not to, saying she already spent enough of her life wondering if her husband and brother would survive it, she didn't want to worry about her little girl too.

I didn't listen. The second I turned eighteen, I signed up. It was my dream and my mother's guilt trips weren't going to stop me. Nothing was.

Sergeant Jensen will.

I shove my arms into the shirt and button it up. By the time I'm done, anyone looking at me would have no idea what just happened. My uniform is neat and exactly as it should be. Random uniform inspections are a real thing and failing one is the *last* thing I need.

"Private Banks?"

I whirl toward the door and see the Private who is scheduled to take over for me. He's new to my unit but he seems like a nice guy. Young, hardworking, focused. He's all the things I was when I enlisted. He's all the things I wish I still was.

"Hi." I finally find the presence of mind to speak.

"Everything okay?" he asks as he looks through the orders for the day.

"Of course," I say, too quickly. "Why wouldn't it be?"

He shrugs. "You were staring at the wall when I came in. I said your name a few times before you even noticed I was here."

So much for Sergeant Jensen being wrong about my erratic behavior.

"Oh, sorry." I take my jacket off the hook by the door. "Just tired, I guess. I, uh, couldn't fall asleep last night."

"Ah, makes sense. Sometimes I can't sleep. Wanna know a trick?"

"Sure."

"Most people will tell you to count sheep or to drink some warm milk. That never worked for me. When I can't sleep, I always start reciting the alphabet backwards. Usually by the third time, I'm out cold."

"I'll keep that in mind."

I straighten my spine and square my shoulders before pushing open the door.

"Have a good…"

The rest of his words trail off the farther down the corridor I get. I push the events of the day to the back of my mind while I walk to the barracks. My roommate won't be there, so I'll have time to shower and wash away the filth that is always there.

After scrubbing myself as clean as humanly possible, I flop down on my mattress and stare at the ceiling. How did I get here? How has my life spun so far out of control that I barely recognize it?

I take a deep breath and close my eyes. It'll be okay, I assure myself. I let the words play on a loop until I almost start to believe them. I can do this. Only two more years and I can get the fuck out of this place.

In the meantime, I'll keep my head down and pray that I get shipped overseas, away from Jensen. Most soldiers like being stationed in the States. Not me. I'd take the middle of nowhere with bullets flying at my head over this any day.

Besides, how much worse can it really get? As I imagine all the ways, my cell phone rings. I roll to my side and pick it up off my nightstand to glance at the screen. It's my mother. I don't really want to talk to her, but I've learned that answering her calls is much easier than dealing with the five-hundred texts that follow when I don't.

"Hi, mom."

"Hi, honey."

She sniffles into the phone and I can tell she's been crying. I sit up and scoot back against the wall, somehow sensing that I'm gonna need something to hold me up.

"Mom? What's wrong?"

"It's Uncle Dusty."

"What about him?"

"He's… he um… oh, honey. He had a heart attack this morning and didn't make it. He's gone."

Numb. A cold and unforgiving numbness settles into my body. I questioned fate and, fickle bitch that she is, called my bluff.

Shit just got worse.

1

LIAM

Present day...

"Don't forget to turn the light off and lock the door on your way out."

I stare at Ruby's bare back and when my fingertips touch her shoulder blade, she curls in on herself. Her reaction is nothing new but expecting it doesn't make me stop trying. Anger hits me so fast that I don't see it coming. I roll away from her to swing my legs over the edge of the bed.

"As if you'd let me forget," I snap.

I stalk around the room to gather up my clothes. The blankets rustle and I glance over my shoulder at her. Ruby is sitting up, with her knees drawn into her chest and her arms wrapped around them. I ignore the urge to sit next to her and ask what's wrong. I tried that the first time I was unceremoniously kicked out of her bed and it did not go well. That was three years ago.

"If you have a problem with our..."

"With our what, Ruby? Spit it out."

She glares at me. "If you have a problem with our *arrangement,* then why do you keep coming back?"

"Honestly?" She nods even though the question is rhetorical. "I have no fucking idea."

I quickly get dressed and after I shove my cell phone in my pocket, I flip the light off and slam the door closed behind me. I'm halfway down the steps when I hear the lock click into place. Shaking my head, I descend the rest of the steps and stride toward my bike in the parking lot.

I straddle the Harley and stare at the building that used to provide me an escape from reality. Dusty's Bar has been a staple in our community since before I was born. It's been the place where the members of the Broken Rebel Brotherhood go to let off a little steam. I didn't even know the tiny apartment above the bar existed until after Dusty died.

My cell vibrates in my pocket before I even get a mile down the road and I pull over to see why. The screen lights up with a text notification and seeing it's from Ruby, I swipe to open it.

U forgot to lock the door

My blood boils at the censure in her words and my grip on the phone tightens until my knuckles are white. My inclination is to ignore her, but my fury won't let me. I shove the phone back into my pocket and turn the bike around.

When I come to a stop at the bottom of the stairs, I kill the engine and force myself to take a few deep breaths to calm down. It doesn't work.

I take the steps two at a time and bang on her door with my fist.

"Ruby!" I shout, grateful the bar isn't in town or near any houses. "Open the damn door."

I continue to pound on the wooden barrier and demand

that she let me in. Just when I'm about to give up, the door swings open.

"What the fuck is your pro—"

My mouth slams shut, and my anger disappears when I see the tear sliding down her cheek. I reach out to wipe it away and she whirls away from the doorway and swipes it away herself.

"What's wrong?" I ask, uncomfortable with the silence.

She doesn't answer me. I step over the threshold, kick the door shut behind me, and close the distance between us. When my hands rest on her shoulders, she flinches. Her reaction to me forgetting to lock the door isn't like her.

Isn't it? You know nothing about her.

Ruby has always seemed like a force of nature. When she took over the bar, a few years after Dusty passed away, she was a no-nonsense boss. She was as green as they come when she arrived, no clue what she was doing, but she learned fast. Really fast. With her in charge, everything runs like a well-oiled machine. She's friendly to the customers and everyone that comes in ends up leaving feeling like they have a new friend.

When she invited me upstairs the day we met to discuss the bar, I had no idea what it would lead to. After our first sexual encounter, I never dreamed it would happen again, but one night, she invited me upstairs for no strings sex—her words, not mine—and I jumped at the chance. Ruby's a gorgeous woman with auburn hair and green eyes that make you feel like she's looking into your soul. She's also a woman with walls stronger than those around Fort Knox.

"Why won't you talk to me?"

"Because," she snaps. "We agreed to no strings. That hasn't changed."

I sigh in exasperation. "That was three years ago, back

when I thought it would be a one-time thing. In case you haven't noticed, it wasn't a one-time thing."

She turns around to face me, the tears gone and in their place a steely determination. "What do you want from me, Liam?"

"Hell, I don't know." That's not entirely true. I know I want more than what she's offering. I want more than she's willing to give. "How about we start with you treating me as more than a damn booty call?"

Her face falls and her shoulders slump. Instead of determination or annoyance, all I see now is pain.

"Just go."

"That's it? That's all you're gonna say?"

"There's nothing else to say." She brushes past me and opens the door. "You need to leave."

"You'd really rather kick me out than talk to me?" I ask, incredulous.

She nods. "This won't happen again."

As I stride past her, I mumble, "I've heard that before." When I make it to my bike, I look back at her and call out, "Next time you wanna fuck, call someone else."

She slams the door in response. It takes me a few minutes to be able to see straight and when I can, I tear out of the parking lot and head home.

The entire drive, I seethe. I think back over the night and wonder where the hell things went wrong. Everything went down like it always does. She closed up the bar and invited me upstairs. I followed and we fucked. Same as usual.

No, not the same. This time, you acted like an ass and changed the rules on her.

When I pull through the gates of the BRB property, I slow the Harley and weave my way over the dirt roads toward my place. I pass the main house, my parent's house, and then the cabin where Cooper and Lila are staying.

That's when it hits me.

Everything was fine with Ruby until the night Isaiah and I took Cooper to Dusty's. Tonight is the first time Ruby's invited me upstairs since that night, the night that everything changed.

That was the night Cooper started asking questions about Ruby and me. That was the night it became apparent to everyone around us that we aren't just casual acquaintances.

2

RUBY

Next time you wanna fuck, call someone else.

Liam's parting words refuse to leave my head. They've taken up residence for the last week and are sticking around like a damn tenant who thinks an eviction order doesn't mean shit.

"Hey, can I get another?"

I stop scrubbing the bartop and force a smile. The man thrusting his mug at me is struggling to stay upright and I know I'm gonna have to call him a cab. I don't recognize the guy but if I had to guess, he's just passing through and he'll be sleeping it off at the motel on the other side of town.

"Sure thing." I grab the mug and fill it from the tap before handing it back to him.

"Thanks," he slurs. He takes a long drink and then wipes his mouth with the back of his hand. "So, you come here often?"

I can't stop the laugh that bubbles up the back of my throat. "I'm the bartender, so yeah."

His eyes drop from my face to my chest. "They were smart when they hired you, ya know that?" He leers at my breasts like he wants to feast on them, and I can't help but shudder under his gaze.

I remind myself that he's drunk and a paying customer, not one of *them*. "If you're waiting on them to respond, it's not gonna happen."

He lifts his head. "What?"

"My tits… they don't talk."

He lifts his mug to his lips and swallows more of the bitter brew. After he sets it back down, he reaches into his pocket and pulls out a twenty, slapping it down in front of me.

"Will they now?"

I narrow my eyes at him and take a few deep breaths. He's lucky I'm already broken because otherwise I'd be slamming his head into the wood. Now, I'm only envisioning myself doing that.

I pull the mug away from him and drop it into the sink under the bar. "I think you've had enough."

"That's not your call to make," he sneers as he stretches his arm out and grabs mine.

Using my free hand, I grab hold of his wrist and twist, causing him to howl in pain. "That's where you're wrong. It is my call."

"You stupid bitch!" he roars, and all eyes turn toward us. Up until this point, the music thumping from the jukebox kept our exchange fairly private but he's taking it to a whole new level now. "Let go of me! I wanna talk to your boss."

"You do? I'm pretty sure you couldn't handle her."

He yanks his arm back and glares. "Let me talk to your—"

"Okay, it's time for you to go."

I shift my eyes to the right and see Liam standing there, hand on the drunk's shoulder. The guy looks at him and seems to deflate.

"Good. Exactly who I wanted to talk to," he says to Liam.

"You need to get your staff under control." He hitches a thumb in my direction. "This bitch took my beer and won't give it back."

Liam looks at me and my mouth goes dry as my tenants make themselves known again.

Next time you wanna fuck, call someone else.

"Aren't you going to do something?" the guy asks. He looks from Liam to me and back again. "Oh, shit. You aren't, are you? She's fucking you so—"

The sound of his head being slammed into the bar is satisfying, but also bad for business. Everyone in town knows who Liam is, knows who the Brotherhood is, but that doesn't mean they want to see them in action while they're relaxing after a long day.

"Liam, it's fine." I force the words past my lips.

He ignores me and lifts the guy's head so he can look him in the eyes. "I think you owe her an apology."

"I don't owe her sh—"

Another deafening thud.

"What was that? I couldn't quite hear you."

Blood pours from the guy's nose and drips onto my floor. His forehead has a gash that will surely require stitches.

"I… I'm sorry."

"For?" Liam prods.

"For being an ass."

Liam looks at me. "That good enough for you?"

It's not but I know it has to be. "Just get him outta here."

Liam drags him away and shoves him out the door. From behind the bar, I see him fall to the ground and scramble to get back up. He turns to come back in, but Liam is standing there with his arms crossed over his chest, blocking his path.

"This isn't over," the guy threatens.

Liam shrugs. "Okay."

I shake my head at them, annoyance creeping in at the

way Liam handled the situation. At the fact that he handled it at all. The twenty dollar bill the guy slapped on the bar catches my eye. I snatch it up and shove it in my pocket. Call it 'hazard pay'.

The other customers return to their drinks and normalcy settles back into the atmosphere. I refill the drinks of the few men at the other end of the bar and try to ignore Liam when he sits on the stool the guy was on.

"Can I get a beer?" he calls out to me after a few minutes.

I walk to stand in front of him and fold my arms over my chest.

"What?" he asks with confusion lacing his tone.

"What the hell was that?"

"I was taking out the trash."

"That's not your job."

Liam's jaw hardens and the corner of his eye twitches. He rests his hands on the wood in front of him and takes a deep breath. "Can't you just say 'thank you' and move on?"

"No, I can't," I snap. "I didn't ask for your help. I had the situation under control."

"Fine. Next time, I'll let whoever it is treat you like shit." He leans forward. "Now, can I please get a beer?"

I grab a bottle and pop the top. "Here." I set it in front of him. "Make it quick and then go."

Liam shrugs and then takes a swig of brew. I busy myself with washing dirty glasses and do my best to ignore his presence.

"Are you okay?"

"Excuse me?"

"You heard me, Ruby." His forehead wrinkles. "Are you okay?"

"I'm fine. Why wouldn't I be?"

"Forget it."

He downs the rest of his beer and tosses a ten-dollar bill

down. Without another word, he walks out of the bar and his Harley roars a minute later. Shame washes through me in his absence.

Liam isn't a bad guy. In fact, he's quite the opposite. But he wants more from me than I'm willing to give, more than I *have* to give.

And the fact that I *almost* want to give it to him is exactly the reason I need to keep him at arm's length.

3

LIAM

"You're seriously not gonna go?"

I roll my neck and grit my teeth. Isabelle, Isaiah and Tillie have been bugging me all day to go hang out at Dusty's tonight and apparently 'no' is not an acceptable answer. Their nagging is making me forget that I actually like them. Growing up in the club together means we have a stronger bond than most but at this precise moment, I don't give a shit about our bond.

"Look, it's been a long day with that new case. I'm just not in the mood."

"You're never 'not in the mood'," Isabelle accuses. "You're always the first one to suggest a night out. What's going on with you?"

"I'm gonna go out on a limb and say it has something to do with a certain redhead."

I glare at Cooper, who's sitting in his chair at the table. We wrapped up our weekly meeting a few minutes ago and he stuck around. I'm glad he's feeling at home and fitting in, but he needs to butt out. He's the one who started this in the first place.

"What about a redhead?" Tillie asks, latching onto Cooper's words.

"There is no re—"

"Wait!" Isabelle braces herself on outstretched arms. "Are you talking about Ruby?"

"Yeah."

"No."

Cooper and I speak at the same time and I heave a sigh.

"Will someone please clue me in on what the fuck is going on?" Isaiah snaps, clearly frustrated that he's not in the loop.

"Nothing is going on." I walk away from them, toward the door, and guilt slams into me. It's not Isaiah's fault that things are all jacked up. It's not his fault that I'm an idiot and let Ruby mean more to me than I ever could to her. It's not his fault that I'm finding a friends with benefits arrangement extremely unsatisfying. I look over my shoulder to repeat my words, but they aren't what comes out of my mouth. "Ruby and I were sleeping together and now we're not. No big deal."

I make my way through the main room and outside, away from prying eyes and nosy friends. I start my Harley and leave them all behind. I ride around for hours, thinking about life, my family, my friends, the club, the newest case… and Ruby.

Why the fuck can't I get her out of my head? We've had fun and we both always walk away satisfied but lately, something has been missing. Maybe it's all the relationship bullshit around me. Everywhere I look, people are happy and settling down. They've got… more.

It's dark by the time I park in front of my house but there's no mistaking Isaiah's form sitting on the steps. When I'm in front of him, he doesn't get up.

"What do you want?" I ask, wanting nothing more than to go inside and fall into bed.

"So... you and Ruby?"

"No, not me and Ruby. I told you, there's nothing there anymore."

Isaiah shoots to his feet. "But there was, and you didn't say anything." His tone screams anger, but his expression tells a whole other story. He's hurt. "Why is that? I'm your best friend and you've said nothing."

"There was nothing to say, Isaiah. It was just sex." I smirk at him. "Do you tell me every time you fuck Tillie?"

"That's not the point, brother," he insists.

"Then what is?"

"Secrets, man. Since when do we keep secrets from each other?"

My control snaps and I get in his face. "Since you left for seven fucking years and started keeping your own. You don't get to judge my decisions."

Isaiah holds his hands up. "Not judging." He turns away from me and walks to the door. "You gonna invite me in for a beer or what?"

"Jesus, you're worse than Ruby," I mutter under my breath as I push past him to unlock the door.

I don't invite him in but that doesn't stop him. It never has and it never will so why even bother?

I grab a beer out of the fridge and toss it at him, annoyed when he catches it with little effort. I swallow down half of mine while I wait for him to talk.

"So, you were sleeping with Ruby and now you're not?"

"Is that a question or are you just repeating my words because you can't come up with your own?"

"Fuck you, asshole," he barks. "I'm trying to understand what the hell is going on. When did you and Ruby hook up?"

When he makes himself comfortable on my couch, with his feet propped on my coffee table, I know I have no choice but to have this conversation. That's the only way I'm going to get him out of my house.

"It started the day she showed up in town."

"Three years ago!" he exclaims and sits up straight. "You've been with Ruby for three years and haven't said a word?"

"To be fair, you weren't here when it started. What was I supposed to do? Write you a letter to tell you I had sex and then wait for you to never respond?"

"That's not what I'm saying at all. I'm just a little floored that in all the time I've been back, you've never once thought to tell me you were dating someone."

"We weren't dating. We were fucking. There's a difference."

"There's a difference when the fucking is a one-time thing… maybe two times. But three years? That's more than fucking."

"Not to her."

"What do you mean?"

"Look, I'm gonna say this once and then we aren't going to talk about it again. Got it?"

"Sure, brother." He grins. "Now spit it out."

"Ruby and I have been sleeping together for a while. Every few months she'd invite me up to her room above the bar and we'd have sex. It was never more than sex. She made it clear early on that she didn't want more." I shove my fingers through my hair. "Fuck and follow her rules. Those were the terms. I did both and now I don't." I shrug. "Maybe she's found someone else. Hell, I don't know."

Liar. You changed the rules on her. You asked her to talk.

"Rules?"

I wave my hand dismissively. "No talking, lights on, she's in control. Shit like that."

Isaiah sits there, curiosity infusing his expression. "Did something happen to end it?"

"No. She just ended it."

"Liam, I may have been gone for seven years but that doesn't change the fact that I know you. Better than anyone else. And you're lying."

"Are you fucking kidding me?"

He rises to his feet. "No, I'm not. Granted, I'm not the only one you're lying to. You're lying to yourself more than anyone else."

"You think you know everything, don't you?" I don't wait for an answer. "I hate to break it to you, but you don't know shit."

"Okay."

I stare at him, frustrated that he can get such a reaction from me because all it's doing is proving him right. I flop down on the couch, not knowing what to say.

"Let me ask you something," he says and sits next to me.

I look at him out of the corner of my eye and give a sharp nod.

"What do you know about Ruby?"

"Not a damn thing! That's the fucking problem."

"I think you should talk to my mom."

"Why the hell would I do that?" I scoff.

"Hear me out," he urges. "When I first met Ruby, she said something about knowing my mom and the BRB."

"So? Everyone knows us. We don't keep ourselves locked away and we don't keep our business a secret. That doesn't mean anything."

"Yeah, maybe. But there was something in the way she said it." He stands back up and walks to the door. "All I'm saying is, maybe there's a reason she has her rules and doesn't want to talk."

When the door shuts behind him, I stay where I'm at, his words echoing in my ears.

Is he right? Does Ruby have the kind of past we see all the time? Is she running from something… someone? I've always had my suspicions but never thought to seek information from anyone other than Ruby. Isaiah's words cause me to have more questions now than I did when I left the bar the other day. So many more questions.

And the answers may be right under my nose, within the club.

4

RUBY

Three years ago...

"Good morning, Fort Bliss. It's gonna be a hot one today as temperatures climb above—"

I turn the radio off and lean back in the driver's seat. I don't give a shit about the weather. Especially for a place that I'm leaving, a place that doesn't want me. I should be happy that it's over, that I've been handed an out that doesn't put my life in jeopardy.

I'm not happy though. Not in the least. I reach across the center console and lift my discharge papers to scan the words again: other designated physical and mental conditions.

That's what the United States Army listed as the reason for discharge. In military speak, it means they don't have a valid reason for kicking me to the curb but can't afford to keep me around. At least, this is how it feels. Discharging me is their way of silencing me, not that a discharge is necessary to do that. Sergeant Jensen made sure I'd never talk.

I toss the papers onto the passenger seat and roll my

neck. I need to get out of here. Now. I put the car in gear and drive out of the parking lot in front of the barracks for the last time. A silent tear trails down my cheek but I swipe it away, telling myself that by doing so, I'm refusing to give in to the overwhelming sense of failure and despair that any human can experience.

I spent the last several days planning out the over twelve-hundred-mile journey to Indiana. When Uncle Dusty died and left his bar to me, I couldn't leave. I had two years left in the military but I'm free now and grateful that I have a place to go. Sure, I could go home to my parents but I'm not the daughter they remember, the daughter they want. I'm damaged, broken, unrecognizable as the girl with big dreams and the attitude to survive anything.

As I drive, my mind wanders to the letter I received after Uncle Dusty's estate was settled. It was from him and I remember sitting in my barracks, my hands shaking as I tore open the envelope. I've read that letter so many times over the last couple of years that I practically have it memorized. I glance toward the passenger seat where the tattered envelope rests. It has given me strength when I thought I had none and I keep it as close as possible, at all times.

My eyes start to feel gritty and my lids heavy. I'm beyond exhausted, as if the years are finally catching up to me. I spot a sign boasting a hotel and I take the exit, grateful to be able to get some sleep.

After checking in, I lug my duffel from the car to the room and toss it on the floor next to the bed. I flop down on the mattress and draw my knees up, resting my feet on the edge. My stomach rumbles, reminding me that I haven't eaten more than a few protein bars since leaving Fort Bliss.

I sit up and snag the laminated hotel fact sheet off the nightstand. I scan through the information until my eyes land on the number for a local pizza joint that delivers. I call to place my order and when they tell me it's going to be forty minutes, I decide to take a quick shower and wash the stink off of me.

Just as I pull my sweats up my legs, there's a knock on the door. I pay for the food and ignore the sleazy look on the acne-faced teenage delivery boy as he stares at my cleavage. He's so focused on my tits that he almost drops the money on the floor.

I let the door slam shut as he walks away and toss the pizza box on the desk, flipping the lid open and grabbing a slice of the cheesy mess. After putting back three pieces, I shut the box and wipe my mouth with a napkin.

I wash my hands and then grab my uncle's letter from my purse. I sit on the bed and scoot back to rest against the headboard as I pull the paper from the envelope and unfold it. The entire routine is familiar, as I've performed it almost every night since receiving it, but it's somehow different. Less calming and more crippling.

My lids slide closed for a brief moment and I suck air into my lungs to work up the courage to read the words. When I'm confident I can get through them without losing my shit, I open my eyes and force them to focus.

Dear Ruby,

If you're reading this, I'm dead.

I chuckle at the bluntness of it. It's just like Uncle Dusty to get right to the point. I curl my legs under me and continue.

First, I want you to know how proud I am of you and your accomplishments. If I had ever been lucky enough to have children of my own, I'd have wanted them to be just like you. You had a dream and you went after it, even when

your parents tried to convince you to do something else, something less dangerous.

Over the years, I watched you grow from a cute, pig-tailed little girl to a woman who knows her mind and knows what she wants in life. But lately, I've watched that same woman slowly disappear into a much smaller, more invisible version of herself.

The wetness that slithers down my cheek hits the corner of my mouth and I lick the saltiness away. I know what's coming next and as much as I don't want to read it, I can't stop myself.

I don't know how to say this, and I've never been known for holding anything back so I'm just going to say it. I think I know what's going on. With you, with them. Our weekly phone calls have morphed into talk of things that I thought I'd left behind when I retired and opened the bar.

I wish I could say that I never saw these kinds of things when I was in the Army, but I'd be lying and one thing I'll never do with you is lie. Unfortunately, I still see this kind of stuff all the time but more on that in a minute.

A tear hits the paper like hundreds of others have done in the past two years, causing the ink to spread. As I have before, I lean my head back and stare at the ceiling, trying like hell to figure out how Uncle Dusty knew. I review phone conversations in my head and come up empty. I never told him about what was happening to me. Shit, I never told a soul after the first failed report.

I shake away my frustration and read on.

By now, you know I've left you the bar. There is no one else in the world I trust to keep it running in the manner in which it has, in a way that keeps it in place for other vets like us to let loose.

But that's not all the bar has to be for you. There's a tiny apartment

above it so it can also provide you a home. The customers are incredible and like no other people I've met. You'll like them… I promise.

I know that you won't leave the military early, so I've ensured that the current staff remains in place and have requested the help of a close friend to keep an eye on the business side of things. His name is Liam Strong.

I snort at the name. I always do. What kind of last name is Strong? Every time I see it, the image that comes to mind is some obnoxiously buff asshole who participates in those bodybuilder competitions on TV.

Liam's a good man and will make sure everything is in order. When you're ready, give him a call and let him know you're coming. He'll be there to greet you and help get you settled. I know you, girly, so stop cussing me out for forcing you into close quarters with a man. Liam is one of the good ones and you can't measure every prick with a penis against those that hurt you.

I let out a watery laugh and my arm falls to the mattress, the letter remaining between my fingertips. I have yet to tell this Liam guy that I'm coming and I'm not sure I will. I never reached out to him, or anyone else at the bar, when Uncle Dusty died and guilt has ridden me hard ever since.

Swinging my legs over the edge of the bed, I set the paper down and go brush my teeth. Tomorrow is going to be a long day and I need sleep if I'm going to get through ten hours of driving. That's how far I need to go if I want to get to the bar on the third day.

When I'm back in bed, I pick up the letter and finish reading.

Ruby girl, I want you to know that there are people here that you can trust, people you can talk to. The motorcycle club that frequents the bar is full of good people, men and women, who can help you get through whatever

baggage you're carrying. Ask Liam about his mom, Brie, and another woman named Sadie. Find them. Talk to them. I promise you won't regret it.

One final thing before this damn arthritis gets the better of my hand. I'm sorry that I never said anything while I was alive. I'm sorry you felt like you couldn't talk to me. I trust you had your reasons and I suspect they stem from nothing good. Keep your chin up and don't let them win. You are so much better than they are, so much stronger than you think.

I love you, Ruby. Always know that, even if you can't talk to me, see me, I'm always with you. Always.

I skip the salutation and read the last words on the page.

P.S. Don't worry… I carried your secret to the grave.

I set the paper on the nightstand and my cell phone catches my eye. I ignore it and crawl under the covers, still unsure if I should call the man my uncle has put into my life. I roll away and stare at the opposite wall, my mind racing. Conversations go through my mind, different possibilities of how it would go if I made the call I'm supposed to make.

After what feels like a lifetime, I twist and reach out to grab the phone. I bring it in front of my face and open up the contacts app. I saved Liam's number after I read the letter the first time. I've stared at it, just as I am now, dozens of times, and always chickened out before using it.

I don't know what the fuck to say. Do I thank him for holding down the fort while I couldn't? Do I tell him that I can handle things without him? What if he didn't do what the letter says and isn't the person my uncle promises him to be? So many questions and zero answers.

Before I can stop myself, I hit the button to send a text message. If there's anything I've perfected while in the military, it's the ability to pretend I'm doing anything else than what I'm actually doing.

My uncle told me you're who I need to contact. I'll be at the bar in two days. Meet me there at 2pm.

I let out a groan as I stare at the sent words. Shit! I type another quick text and hit send before tossing the phone back onto the nightstand and pulling the blanket over my head.

This is Ruby.

5

LIAM

Three years ago...

I tip the beer bottle back and finish it off. The reports in front of me are a fucking mess and I've been trying to make sense of them for a few hours now. I tap the bar and the bartender sashays her way to me.

"Can I get another, Cindy?"

"Sure thing."

Cindy has been handling the books for Dusty's Bar while I was at college. I made a point to check in every few months when I was home, but I'm back for good now and apparently, it's not soon enough. When Cindy pops the top of the fresh bottle and sets it in front of me, I nod my thanks and keep skimming through numbers.

My cell lights up and I slide it toward me to see why. A text comes through and I don't recognize the number, so I ignore it and force myself to keep going with the reports. When it lights up again a few minutes later and I read that notification, a calm rage begins to simmer.

This is Ruby.

I reread the first text and my eyes narrow at the words on the screen. She can't be serious. I hear nothing from this chick in two years and now she's issuing demands. Fuck that!

My pulse pounds in sync with the beat of the music blaring from the jukebox. Not only do I not want to deal with Dusty's niece, but I don't even know how to teach her the financial side of the business when I'm struggling with it. Why Dusty put me in charge of the books is a mystery and one I'll likely never have an answer to.

That's not true. He told you why.

My anger subsides as a sudden urge to read the letter Dusty left me hits. I snatch the reports up and shove my cell into my back pocket. I keep the letter in my top dresser drawer at home. I tell myself that's not the only reason I'm leaving the bar. I need a quiet place to focus on these spreadsheets and home is the only place I'm likely to get that. I wave to Cindy as I head toward the door and she smiles back.

My Harley is parked by the streetlight at the edge of the parking lot, and I straddle her. The ride home does little to calm me, and when I step inside, I pull out my cell and read the text from Ruby again.

Two days. I've got two days to figure out the mess Cindy's made, to redo the books so they're easy to understand and user friendly. I run up to my loft office space, snag my laptop off the desk, and carry it back down to the couch. I drop it onto a cushion and then head toward my bedroom.

You know what the letter says. No need to read it... again.

I ignore the voice in my head and yank open the drawer. Lifting up pairs of socks and boxer briefs, I spot the envelope on the bottom in the back. I pull it out and put it between my teeth as I shed my boots and jeans. My T-shirt is next and when I'm finally comfortable, I head back out to the living room.

After flopping down on the couch, I open the envelope and begin to read.

Dear Liam,

If you're reading this, I'm dead. Go ahead, grab a shot and absorb the news… I'll wait.

I let out a laugh at the absurdity of Dusty's words. He was always a funny guy and even in death, that didn't change.

I've spent the last few weeks writing letters to the people in my life, knowing my time was coming, and this is the last one. If the words are a little messy, forgive me. Arthritis is a bitch. Never get old… it sucks.

By now, I'm sure you know that I left my bar to my niece. Unfortunately, she's still in the Army and can't just hop on a plane and come running just because my old heart decided it was time. That's where you come in.

I've asked Cindy and the other staff to stay on and they all agreed to it before I kicked the bucket. I know the place will run smoothly and they can handle the day-to-day stuff, but business people they are not.

I think back to the first time Cindy tried to go over the financials with me and she had no clue about profit and loss. She's phenomenal with the customers and can mix a mean drink but she's clueless about business.

Liam, I need a favor. You are the only person I know, other than your dad, who's good with computers and numbers. I'd ask your dad but we both know his hands are full with the club. Yours will be too, sooner rather than later, but you're younger and can handle both.

Anyway, I'm rambling like the old man that I am. I need you to keep an eye on the financial aspect of the bar, keep the books, make sure the bills get

paid. I need this place to be here for Ruby when she leaves the military. I trust you to ensure that happens.

The corners of my mouth lift into a smile. I don't know what I did to deserve Dusty's trust, but I'm as determined now as I was the first time I read this letter to not disappoint him.

Ruby has a few years left with the Army and she won't be re-upping. My niece always dreamed of being in the military, serving her country like her father and I did. Sometimes dreams aren't at all what we expect, and I worry she's learning that the hard way.

Enough of that. I would be eternally grateful if you could do this for me. And if you could meet with Ruby when she does come, teach her everything she needs to know, I promise not to haunt you.

Ruby is an amazing young woman and I know you'll treat her with respect and kindness. The kid needs it and I suspect she'll need it even more when she's out.

I pull out the pictures that were included with the letter. They're old and faded but they capture moments of a little girl's childhood that I imagine was happy and full of love and laughter. As it always does when I look at them, my stomach twists and my heart cracks.

The thought of anyone making this child learn something the hard way is gut wrenching. I know that I didn't have the most charmed life growing up around all of the problems that come to the Broken Rebel Brotherhood, but I haven't known anything else. This child knew nothing but goodness and now? Who knows?

In my letter to Ruby, I included your phone number so she can keep you posted on when she expects to be here. My hope is that you two have the chance to talk before that happens, get to know each other. Please don't

change your number. I'd hate for her to reach out and some lunatic creep answer because they recycled the phone number. Did you know they do that? Stupid if you ask me.

One last favor before I go. When Ruby does show up, don't ask a ton of questions. I have no idea what kinda shape she'll be in, but I know my girl. She won't stick around if she feels like she's being grilled and I need her to stick around. I need her to make this place her home because I know she'll be safe here. Don't take that from her. Don't take her safety and security.

I know you're probably wondering why she needs safety or why she can't go home to her parents for that. And I'm sorry I'm leaving you without answers. But I know you'll do the right thing. I've watched you grow up and you've turned into a fine young man. I trust you. Hell, I'm trusting you with the one thing that I don't trust many people with… my niece.

Thank you, Liam. Thank you for making it possible for an old man to die knowing that things will be okay.

-Dusty

P.S. Piece of advice… invite your mom and Sadie to the bar when Ruby arrives. That'll help more than I can say.

I toss the letter and pictures onto the coffee table and put my feet up. I can't get my mind off of the words Dusty wrote. He didn't say much but at the same time, he said a lot. He's right, I've got questions. A ton of them.

I link my fingers behind my head and lean back to stare at the ceiling. Two days. That's it. Two days until maybe, just maybe, I can get some answers.

I shake the thought from my head. I won't get answers in two days. Not if Dusty's assumption about Ruby not talking is correct. I'll do what he asked. I won't fish for information. And I'll do everything in my power to make sure she feels safe and secure. I'll do whatever it takes to make her see that she has friends, even among people she doesn't know.

Two days.

6

RUBY

Present day...

"Hey, Ruby, you've got a phone call!"

I look up from my task and glance at Cindy, who's standing at the other end of the bar holding out the corded phone for me. I stride toward her and grab the phone to put up to my ear.

"This is Ruby," I say into the receiver.

"Ruby Banks?"

My defenses immediately go up. Anyone who has the bar's phone number knows I'm the only Ruby here and wouldn't need to confirm my last name. "Who is this?"

"My name is Eileen," the caller says. She sounds young and her voice is hushed, like she doesn't want her call to be overheard. "We've never met, but I'm stationed at Fort Bliss, under Douglas Jensen."

I didn't even know I was holding my breath until it whooshes out of me in a rush. My stomach cramps and I struggle to breathe.

"I'm sorry to call you like this but I'm hoping you can help me."

Somehow, I find my voice. "I can't help," I say flatly.

"I think you can," Eileen insists. "Look, I didn't know who else to call but I need your—"

I slam the phone into its cradle, unable to listen to whatever she has to say. If she's tracking me down and she's familiar with Jensen, it can't be anything good.

The room starts to spin, and I grip the edge of the bar to steady myself. I look around at the customers, almost as if searching for Jensen himself to be there.

"Rubes, you okay?"

A hand rests on my shoulder and I whirl around, arms flailing to rid myself of the contact.

"Don't fucking touch me!" I shout.

Cindy's eyes widen and her hands go up, as if to protect herself from me. Pinpricks dance along the back of my head telling me I'm being stared at. I swallow past the lump in my throat, the shame that comes on the heels of one of my outbursts. Tears burn at the back of my eyes, but I manage to hold them at bay.

"Cindy, I'm sorry. I didn't mean..." I shake my head, unable to continue.

"Hey, Rubes, it's fine." Her voice is reassuring but it does little to sooth me. "Why don't you take the rest of the night off? I can handle closing tonight."

Her offer swirls around in my brain but I dismiss it quickly. "No." I shake my head. "No, I'm good." If I leave, he wins... again.

"Are you sure? I really don't mind."

"Yeah, I'm sure." I force a smile. "Thanks anyway."

"Will you at least take a break? Grab something to eat or whatever. You look like you're gonna pass out."

I give a curt nod and make my way around the bar and

through the swinging door that leads to the kitchen. Sonny, the cook, waves at me with a spatula in his hand. I lift my hand in greeting and when I hit the back stairs that'll take me to my apartment, I take them two at a time.

Behind the security of my apartment door, I lean against the wall and let out the sadness and the shame and the anger that's begging to be unleashed, that's always just under the surface waiting to be triggered. Tears stream down my cheeks and when they hit my lips, I lick them away as if swallowing the salty emotions will somehow eliminate them forever. I should know better though.

I've done the same thing dozens of times and all it does is force me to absorb the emotions into my soul for all eternity. But for a brief moment in time, I soak up the purging of everything negative within me. I allow myself to feel cleansed, to feel better.

You're far from better.

I swipe the last of the wetness from my face and push off the wall. I don't bother turning on the one overhead light I have and opt for a little night light I keep plugged in on the kitchen wall. I glance around the tiny apartment that I've called home for the last few years. The compact size has always comforted me somehow, made me feel safe, but now it only makes me feel claustrophobic and confined.

I pull some lunch meat out of the fridge and make myself a sandwich. I'm not hungry but I know that Cindy is right. I need to eat. Forcing food down my throat is nothing new. In the Army, we ate when we were told to eat, hungry or not, and we never complained because we knew that we had to keep up our strength.

I toss my napkin in the trash can under the sink and then turn on the faucet to splash cold water onto my face. As I'm drying my skin on a clean dish towel, there's a knock on my door. My entire body stiffens with tension and my heart skips a beat. For a moment, I'm back on base and waiting for the Devil himself to enter.

The knock becomes an incessant banging, but I can't force my feet to move. The pounding seems to shift from the wooden barrier to inside my skull. This can't be happening. He can't be here. How did he find me?

"Ruby, open the damn door!"

The voice on the other side of security is deep, raspy, and... worried? No, that can't be right. I'm the one who should be worried. My hands begin to shake and the apartment walls ripple like a flag blowing in the wind. I manage to take a step toward the door, but my knees wobble and the voice starts to fade into the distance.

"Dammit Ruby! Don't make me break..."

Pain splinters through my head when it bounces off the floor and I'm thrown into darkness.

~

Liam

Ten minutes earlier...

I stare at the sign above the door of Dusty's bar and shove my fingers through my hair. I don't know why I came here tonight other than I simply couldn't stay away. I had to see her. Fuck, I need to *feel* her, but I'll settle for whatever I can get.

I swing my leg over my Harley and take a deep breath. My brain hollers at me to get back on my bike and go home or go to a different bar and find a different woman. But I don't. I can't. Ruby is the only woman for me, despite our *unconventional* relationship.

There is no relationship.

For Ruby, that's true. There is nothing more between us than occasional sex and even that is over… I think. But there hasn't been another woman since the first day she walked into Dusty's Bar and that's exactly how I want things to stay.

I push through the door and my eyes land on Ruby and Cindy behind the bar. Cindy's hands are up, and her eyes are wide. I can only see Ruby from behind, but her posture is rigid, which is in stark contrast with her flailing arms.

What the fuck?

I watch them talk for several minutes, unable to take my eyes off of the scene before me. I can't hear what they're saying over the music but when Ruby shoves through the door to the kitchen, I know it's nothing good.

I weave through the tables and sit on a stool at the far end of the bar. I wait a few minutes for Cindy to finish getting a beer for the guy at the other end, and when she walks toward me, I smile.

"Hey, stranger," she greets me. "What can I get ya?"

"What was that all about?" I ask nodding toward the direction Ruby took off in.

Cindy leans forward, as if it's a secret. "I don't even know, Liam," she starts. "She got a phone call and looked pretty upset. I tried to talk to her, but she flipped out. I convinced her to go grab some food but I gotta say, I wish she'd just take the night off."

"Phone call?"

"Yeah, some woman." Cindy shrugs. "No clue who it was and I'm pretty sure I'll never know. Ruby isn't exactly the sharing kind."

"No shit," I mumble.

"What?"

"Nothing." I heave a sigh. "Maybe I should go check on her."

Even as the words leave my mouth, I know it's a stupid

idea. It's not like Ruby will talk to me. She has her rules, after all, and checking on her will only serve one purpose: push Ruby further away than she's always been. And even as all the warning bells jangle in my mind, I know I'm going to ignore them.

"That'd be great, Liam," Cindy agrees. "You're the only person she'll talk to."

Is that really what people think? That Ruby and I are such great friends and that I hold some sort of special place in her life? Ha! I wish.

"I doubt she'll talk to me, but I'll try."

I slide off the stool and head back outside and around the building to the steps. I've never gone uninvited up to Ruby's apartment via the back entrance and I'm certain she wouldn't appreciate me starting to now.

I walk up the stairs and knock lightly on the door. Something freaked Ruby out and I have no intention of adding to that. There's no answer

Walk away. Get back on your bike and forget about her. She doesn't want you. She doesn't need you.

Tension builds in my muscles. I roll my neck and blow out a breath. I lift my fist and knock again, this time a little harder. When there's still no answer, I call out to her.

"Ruby, open the damn door!"

I press my ear to the wood and listen for any sign that she's still inside. I don't hear anything, but I'm not convinced. I pull my cell phone out of my back pocket and send her a text.

Ruby, are u in there?

I stare at my phone for several minutes until those three dots appear. Air rushes past my lips with the breath I didn't even know I was holding.

This is Cindy. She left her phone in the bar. She's not back.

My stomach drops. Shit! Instead of knocking, I pound on her door, demanding she let me in. Worry spreads through me like tiny little spiders making themselves at home in my blood. I hear the floor creak with movement inside.

"Dammit, Ruby, don't make me break the door—" Thud. "—down."

My heart skips several beats as I back up on the landing. The flimsy wooden door splinters as my booted foot kicks it in. Ruby is lying on the floor and I rush forward, dropping onto my knees beside her.

Blood oozes from a gash on her temple and I press my hand over the wound to staunch the bleeding. I glance around the apartment as if the space will give me the answers to all of my looming questions. Surprise, it doesn't.

When the bleeding seems to slow, I remove my hand and lift Ruby into my arms. I carry her to the bed and lay her down on the sheets. She doesn't stir. I gently shake her, trying to get a response.

"Ruby, it's me." I roll my eyes at myself. Ruby's unconscious and can't hear me. But don't doctors tell people to talk to someone who's in a coma? This is similar, right? She can hear me. She *has* to hear me.

"C'mon, Ruby love, wake up for me."

7

RUBY

"C'mon, Ruby love, wake up for me."

Ruby love?

Why is someone in my apartment? My eyes flutter open and I immediately slam them shut against the light. I don't remember turning it on, but I must have.

"Ah, there you are."

My lids fly open again and my gaze lands on Liam. I shoot up from my prone position and instantly regret it when a wave of nausea hits me. I groan and fall back to the bed.

"What are you doing here?" I ask with as much annoyance as I can muster.

"I stopped by the bar and saw you leave." The mattress shifts as Liam gets up. "Cindy was worried and asked me to check on you."

I feel the loss of his body heat and roll my neck so I can look at him. He's pacing and his muscles are tense. I know what would ease that tension, but I don't let my mind go there. After several minutes of silence, he stops next to me and looks at me with worry creasing his forehead.

"Who called you?"

"What?"

"Dammit, Ruby, you heard me." His jaw tics with frustration. "Who was on the phone and why did they send you running?"

"None of your business," I snap.

I try to sit up again, slowly, and when my stomach doesn't do a cartwheel, I swing my legs over the side of the bed and plant my feet. I grip the edge of the mattress with both hands and push myself up, swaying slightly.

Liam grabs my arm to help steady me and drops his hand to his side when I stiffen. I put one foot in front of the other and start to walk away.

"Where are you going?" he asks from behind me.

Without stopping, I answer. "The bathroom. I want to see the gash I can feel on my temple." I absently lift my arm and touch it with my fingertips, wincing at the sting.

After I flip on the bathroom light, I push the door closed. Not for the first time, I wish there was a lock on this particular door. Who doesn't put a lock on a bathroom door?

I lean my palms onto the counter and look at my reflection in the mirror. Dried blood is caked in my hair, as well as my cheek. I grab a clean washcloth off of the shelf above the toilet and run it under cold water. Just as I place the damp cloth to the cut, the door swings open. I try to kick my leg out to stop it but with no luck.

"Here," Liam says as he snags the cloth away from me. "Let me."

I glare at him and when he arches a brow, I huff out a breath and cross my arms over my chest.

"Sit down," he orders and tips his head to indicate the toilet.

Every single cell in my body wants to defy the order, to stand my ground and do whatever the hell I want. But the pain from the gash reminds me that it needs cleaned and possibly stitched up. It'll be easier for someone else to take care of it than it will be for me to do it myself.

"Was that so hard?" he quips when I sit.

"Yes."

Liam chuckles. "You have got to be the most stubborn woman I've ever met."

"Thank you."

He shakes his head and continues to chuckle. "I'm not sure that was a compliment." Liam pulls the now blood-stained cloth from my face and runs it under warm water to rinse it off. "Do you have any antiseptic and bandages? Butterfly bandages would be best."

I scoff. "I'm an Army vet. Of course I've got that stuff." I point to the bottom drawer in the vanity. "In there."

"Right."

Liam bends at the knees and tugs the drawer open. He rifles through the contents until he finds what he's looking for. When he rises to his full height, my stomach flip-flops and not in the way it did earlier when I thought I was going to puke. Liam is sex personified and I'm woman enough to admit that he gets to me on a very primal level.

He dabs at the cut a few more times and then applies the antiseptic. I wince at the sting and he blows on it to ease the pain. My eyes slide closed as his breath caresses my skin and I can almost forget that I don't want him here. Almost.

"You're lucky this doesn't need stitches," he says quietly. "The bandages should do the trick, but I can take you to the ER if you wanna be sure."

"No." I shake my head. "No ER."

"Okay."

Liam finishes tending to my temple and when he's done, he simply stands there and stares at me.

"What?" I snap.

"Nothing." He shakes his head and turns to walk out of the room. Instead of crossing the threshold, he stops and looks over his shoulder. "Would it really be so bad to let someone in a little? To let *me* in?"

I don't have time to respond before he disappears around the corner. My shoulders sag and I wait for my apartment door to open and close. When it doesn't, I'm surprised... and inexplicably happy.

"I'm not leaving, Ruby, so you might as well come out of there and face me."

Liam's tone conveys resignation and a little determination. I smile at the combination but school my features before I enter the main room of my apartment and face him. He's leaning against the counter, legs stretched out and crossed at the ankles. His muscles are bulging beneath his T-shirt and I swallow past the lump in my throat.

"Are you going to answer my question?" he asks when I stop in front of him.

"Which one?"

"Take your pick."

I think back over the questions he's asked me since I woke up. I don't want to answer any of them so I ask one of my own instead.

"Why did you call me 'Ruby love'?"

He huffs out a breath and drops his gaze to stare at the floor. He shrugs. "It just came out."

"Love is a pretty powerful word to *just come out.*"

"Yeah, sure, if I meant anything by it. I didn't so you can stop worrying."

"I'm not worried," I lie. I open the fridge and pull out a beer. "You want one?"

"Am I going to be here long enough to drink it?"

I shrug. "That's up to you."

Liam's head whips in my direction and his eyebrows

shoot up in surprise. "Yeah, I'll take one." I hand it to him. "Thanks," he says as he twists the cap off.

We both stand there, silent and drinking the cold Bud Light. When he tosses his empty bottle in the trash under the sink, it clanks with a few other empty bottles, the sound startling me.

"Ruby, we need to talk."

"Do we?" I counter.

He stares at me as if trying to make up his mind about something. "Forget it."

Liam stomps to the door and yanks it open. He glances over his shoulder and the hurt in his eyes shatters me. I won't admit it out loud, but I can't let him leave. Not like this.

"Wait," I call just before he pulls the door closed.

He turns around to face me but says nothing.

I drop my gaze and swallow. When I lift my head, I force a smile. "Thank you."

"For what?" He shuts the door and remains inside. "For picking your ass up off the floor, for cleaning up your head, for fucking you for the last few years, for following your rules, or for leaving so you don't have to talk?"

His words burn like acid, but I deserve them. Every single one. He's not going to like my answer but at least it's the truth.

"All of it."

8

LIAM

All of it.

My eye twitches and my blood boils.

"Wrong fucking answer."

Ruby's eyes widen. "What?"

"You heard me." I stalk toward her and when I'm inches away, I stop and lean close. "Wrong. Fucking. Answer."

"But…"

But what?" I snarl. When she says nothing, I fling my arms wide. "You really don't get it, do you?"

"Get what?" she cries.

"Forget it."

I whirl away from her and begin to pace. I was ready to leave, to walk out and try to forget she even exists but that's not what I want. I certainly don't want to fight with her, but I can't seem to stop myself from provoking exactly that.

"No, I won't forget it." She reaches out to grab my arm and stop me, but I move away so she misses. "Liam, stop pacing." Ruby lifts her hands to rub her temples and winces when she touches the butterfly bandages. "Shit!" She tilts her head back and blows out a breath. "Why was that the wrong answer?"

I ignore the question for as long as I can. Which apparently, is not all that long because several seconds later, I'm stopped in front of her again, bent close to whisper in her ear.

"You don't need to thank me for fucking you, love," I growl, and she shivers.

"But you said—"

"I know what I said," I bark and then nip at her neck because I can't help it. "I'm pissed. People say stupid shit when they're pissed."

I lick a path over the spot I nipped and Ruby whimpers.

"You like that?"

"Mmmm."

I tug her shirt to expose her shoulder and my tongue follows. Ruby leans into my touch, silently begging for more. I yank her shirt over her head and my cock jumps at the sight of her perfect, perky tits, which aren't concealed behind a bra.

I pause to look my fill. When she lifts her hands to cover herself, I wrap my fingers around her wrists to stop her.

"Don't," I whisper roughly.

"I thought you didn't want to do this anymore."

"I didn't," I confirm. "I don't." When her eyes widen, I rush to clarify. "Ruby, I want more than a quick fuck with you, but my dick hasn't gotten the memo."

I lift my hand and run a fingertip down her cheek, toward her lips. She sucks the finger into her mouth, swirling her tongue around it. My eyes roll into the back of my head and my legs begin to shake with need.

I pull my finger out from between her lips and trail it over her chin, down her neck and circle a pebbled nipple. Ruby takes several steps away from me, her eyes never leaving mine. She grips the waist of her pants and slides them over her hips and down her legs, taking her panties off in the process.

When she's naked before me, she arches a brow. "Are we gonna do this?"

The signals between my brain and my heart scramble and I rush to strip my clothes. When I'm as naked as she is, I close the distance between us and lift her up. She wraps her legs around my waist, and I crash my mouth into hers.

The kiss is rough, savage, sinfully hot. I back her into the wall, my weight holding her up. I pin her arms above her head and link my fingers with hers.

"Are you sure?" I ask.

Rather than answer, Ruby arches her back as best she can in her position, her warm pussy pressing against my cock. I shift to hold her wrists with one hand and reach between us to fist my dick and guide it toward her opening.

I thrust forward and Ruby's head thuds back against the wall. I piston in and out of her. My movements are fast, hard, frantic. Our lips fuse together, and I swallow her moans while she inhales my grunts.

There is nothing sweet or loving about the way we fuck. There never is but this time is different. Animalistic. Angry. Desperate.

Sweat slicks our bodies and slapping skin, along with unintelligible mumblings, are the only sounds to fill the space.

"Come for me, love," I growl into her ear and then sink my teeth into her neck.

Ruby freezes for a moment and I fear I crossed a line. I didn't mean to. I have no control where she's concerned, and the word just slipped out. I settle my hand between us and press my thumb into her clit in an effort to refocus her attention. That little bit of pressure is all it takes for her to match my thrusts and forget the words that came out of my mouth.

"That's it. Come on my cock."

"Ah, fuck… oh shit…"

"I'm gonna come, Ruby," I snarl and increase my speed. "Are you coming with me?"

One more thrust and her walls clamp down. As she spasms around me, my own pleasure ricochets through me and my muscles tense up with my release.

Our movements slow and she falls limp in my arms. Unable to hold her up any longer, I carry her to the bed, and we bounce on the mattress when I fall back, Ruby still in my arms. We lie there for a few moments, both panting, neither of us saying a word.

Ruby tilts her head and looks into my eyes. I can't tell what she's thinking, and I want to ask. I don't though. I'm afraid of the answer. I'm terrified that it won't be anywhere close to what's going through my head. It won't be that what we have is incredible. It won't be that she wants more. It won't be what I want.

Ruby rises from the bed and grabs her clothes off the floor. She silently gets dressed, all the while avoiding my gaze, avoiding the unasked questions.

"You know this changes nothing, right?" she asks over her shoulder from her spot in front of the door.

Rage simmers just beneath the surface. My muscles coil so tight it's painful. When I don't respond, she drops her gaze to the floor for a second. She lifts her head, smiles sadly at me and walks out without another word, pulling the door shut behind her and leaving me alone, angry, *hurt*.

She's wrong that this changes nothing. Everything has changed.

The problem is, I'm not exactly sure how.

9

RUBY

"That woman called again."

My brows knit together but I don't look at Cindy. We're doing inventory at the bar and I need to remain focused on the spreadsheets on my laptop, not the eleven unwanted phone calls over the past week or thoughts about my past.

"Thirty-three cases of Bud Light," she says.

She waits a second for me to type in the number and then shuts my laptop, forcing me to glance up.

I blow out a breath. "What?"

"Rubes, I don't know who this woman is or what she wants but I gotta tell ya..."

Cindy fidgets with her hands and then shoves them in her pockets. Her eyes narrow and she looks uncomfortable. Uncomfortable but determined.

"Spit it out, Cin."

"It's just... I don't know. She sounds scared."

"I'm sure she is," I concede.

"But why? Who is she?"

I slide off the stool and walk around the bar to pour a shot. I lift an extra glass, silently asking Cindy if she wants one too and she nods. I pour us both a shot of Jack Daniels and empty mine down my throat before she can even lift hers.

I flatten my palms on the bar and lean forward. "Cindy, I like you. You're more than just an employee. You're my friend. But I'm only going to say this once so listen up." I pause to make sure she's really listening. "The phone calls, the woman and what she wants, are not up for discussion. I don't want to talk about it. If I have to say that again, you're fired. Got it?"

Cindy's eyes widen and her face hardens. She slams her glass down, the sound like a clap of thunder. "Got it," she says with a bite in her tone. "But Rubes, that's not friendship. Friends talk. Friends share. Friends lean on each other. Clearly, we're not friends so quit pretending otherwise and I'll do the same."

I stare at her back as she storms out of the bar, the door slamming shut behind her and my body deflates. I hate that my instinct is to push people away, good people who deserve better than what I have to offer.

I don't have time to dwell on it though because liquor bottles and cases of beer aren't going to count themselves. I push off the bar and force myself to methodically work my way through the task. I manage to finish up with two hours to spare before I have to open the bar.

With a little time on my hands and my laptop tucked under my arm, I head upstairs to my apartment. I need to order refills on my prescriptions and that's not something I ever do while in the bar. I even opened a PO box so they wouldn't be delivered where anyone can see them.

I set my laptop on the counter and grab a Coke from the

fridge. I pull up the VA's ordering system and just as my cursor hovers over the checkbox next to 'Zoloft', a notification flashes on the screen letting me know I have a new email. Without looking at it, I finish my order and then switch to the email app.

My stomach bottoms out when I see who the email is from: Eileen Dorsey. How the hell did she get my email address? I read the subject line and bile rises up the back of my throat. **Please help me.** Three little words that used to have an effect on me, one that would trigger a response I could be proud of. Now, those words have me contemplating packing everything I own and hitting the road, running before shit can hit the fan.

I take a few swallows of my pop, wishing it was mixed with a little rum—okay, a lot of rum—so I could numb the emotions fogging my brain. I stare at the computer screen, debating whether or not to open the email or delete it and pretend it never existed.

My conscience wins and I open the email. There's no one here to witness my reaction and ask questions. And while that's true, I can't help the little twinge of longing, the voice in my head that is wishing Liam were here. To do what, I have no idea. I only know that his presence would make it somehow tolerable.

I take a deep breath and read the words in front of me.

Ruby,

I apologize for the email, but you won't take my phone calls and I really need your help. I am currently stationed at Fort Bliss. I was excited to join the Army and serve our country but it's turned into a nightmare that I can't escape. You see, I was assigned to work under Douglas Jensen.

My muscles coil at the name and my vision becomes

hazy. I don't want to think about Jensen, but Eileen is determined to make me.

Jensen is a disgrace to the military. He's arrogant, rude, demanding, and a sexual predator. He has raped me for months. I tried to report it but that didn't go as planned.

Flashbacks of my monthly *visits* from Jensen assault me from every direction until the memories have beaten my mind bloody. My lungs seize up and breathing becomes almost impossible. Sweat beads on my forehead and the room spins around me, threatening to suck me into a void.

I lean on the counter to ground myself in the present and count to a hundred. Panic attacks are nothing new to me and I've learned how to regain control. It doesn't always work but fortunately, today it does. When my breathing stabilizes and I no longer feel as if I'm going to pass out, I refocus my attention on the email.

I know you went through something similar. Don't ask me how I know… I just do. That's a conversation for another time.

Anyway, I've managed to track down two other victims—Leslie and Denise—and I'm sure there are more. The problem is, the military is doing everything in their power to ignore the problem.

Here's where you come in. They can pretend that rape isn't happening right under their noses when it's one woman but when we band together, we'll be impossible to ignore. I want to take this asshole down. I want to make him pay for what he's done to me and to you and to who knows how many others.

So, will you help me? Will you tell your story? I've found an attorney who's willing to listen and point us in the right direction but he's made it pretty clear that there is power in numbers.

I know this is asking a lot and I'm sorry for that but I don't know what else to do. Jensen is going to keep raping female subordinates as long

as his pecker is still working. While it would be more satisfying to Lorena Bobbitt his ass, I'll settle for stripping him of his power, of his military status and credentials. I'll settle for making him pay within the confines of the law.

I can't stop the smile that plays on my lips at her determination. I'd love to bring Jensen down. I just don't know if I can. I'm not sure I'll survive reliving the terror he put me through, not to mention the threats he made to keep me quiet.

If you decide you don't want to help, I guess I'll have to respect that and you won't hear from me again, but if you decide to help, you can reach me at 915-555-7774. Don't worry, that number is secure, as is the server I sent this email from. I know Jensen's proclivity for threats and wouldn't put you in jeopardy like that.

I really hope you reach out. If not for me, or even for yourself, then for the hundreds of other women out there who have experiences that mirror our own... not just with Jensen but throughout the military.

Sincerely,

Eileen Dorsey

I heave a sigh and make my way to the couch, flopping down and leaning my head against the back. What the hell am I supposed to do? It's one thing to live my life and pretend that what happened to me didn't happen. It's another thing entirely to try to pretend it's not happening to others... lots of others.

You know what you have to do.

I don't know the precise moment my mind makes itself up for me but what's done is done. I have to do something. Like Eileen said, if not for me then for the others. I just hope I can separate the two.

Decision made, I reach into my back pocket for my cell

phone. I pull up the texting app and scroll until I find the name I'm looking for. I type a quick message.

I think I need your help.

Without allowing myself time to second guess my action, I hit send.

10

LIAM

"She said she's not working tonight."

I lift my head and shift my gaze to the left. Isaiah is standing there, arms crossed over his chest and a smug look on his face. I've been sitting at the bar for two hours, nursing one beer after the other, hoping to drown my sorrows. It hasn't worked.

"Okay."

Isaiah drops his arms to his sides. "What the fuck, man?"

I narrow my eyes and glare. "What?"

"You've been stuck on this girl for how long and you're finally given an opening, and this is how you react? I don't get it."

"Finally given an opening?" I ask, incredulously. "So all the fucking we've done wasn't 'opening' enough?" I shake my head and return my attention to my beer, rolling the bottle between my hands.

Isaiah sits down on the empty stool next to me and raises a finger to let Cindy know he wants a drink. When she sets a cold bottle in front of him, he snags it and takes a long pull.

"So," he begins when he's finished the beer. "I'm gonna say this and what you decide to do with it is up to you."

He pauses and looks at me, as if expecting me to argue. When I don't, he continues.

"Fucking is just that… it's fucking. From what you've told me, which admittedly hasn't been a lot, she told you from the get-go that that's all it would ever be." He slides his empty bottle toward the edge of the bar for Cindy to grab as she walks by and stands. I turn my head to look at him. "Now she's asking for the club's help." He slaps me on the back. "Dude, you're the goddamn club."

Isaiah walks away, leaving me to consider his words. He's wrong. She asked for the club's help and I'm a member of the club, yes, but she didn't come to me. Not when it mattered. She's pushed me away and maintained her walls for so long that I'm not even sure she would know how to be any different.

You are the club.

I sit up straight, Isaiah's voice ricocheting through my mind.

You are the club. You are the club. You are the club.

Damn right I'm the club.

I flatten my palms on the bar and leverage myself up so fast my stool almost topples to the floor. Cindy spares me a glance, eyebrows raised. I shove my hand in my pocket and grab a few bills to toss down onto the bartop. I nod at her and she smiles.

I stride out the front door and around the side to the steps that will take me to Ruby. Isaiah isn't wrong. She asked for the club's help and I am the club. So, I'm going to be the one to help her. Or at the very least, she's going to talk to me. No more walls. No more rules. No more secrets.

I take the steps two at a time and the rock music blaring

through her apartment door drowns out all other sound. I pound on the door, hard enough so she'll hear me and take a step back to wait. The only response I get is the music being cranked up a few notches. It's a good thing there's a constantly playing jukebox in the bar or she'd be driving her customers nuts.

I pound on the door again, a little harder and yell through the barrier, "Ruby, it's me. Let me in."

Still, nothing. I reach down and turn the knob, finding it unlocked. I debate for a split second about whether it's smart to just barge in, but then I remember why I came up here. I twist the knob and shove the door open.

Ruby is in the middle of her tiny living space, dancing to the music in nothing but a skimpy pair of underwear and a bra. My cock immediately springs to life and before she notices me, I adjust myself. I stand there, silently watching her, mesmerized by her body, her curves... her.

"Take a picture, it'll last longer," she calls over her shoulder and then struts to the stereo and stabs the off button with a finger. When she turns to face me, she folds her arms over her chest, pushing her tits almost to the point that they spill out over the lacy cups. "What do you want, Liam?"

I swallow down all of the saliva that's pooled in my mouth at the sight of her. "I, uh..." I run a shaky hand through my hair and take a few deep breaths. "We need to talk."

Her arms fall to her sides and she stares at me for a moment before walking to her bed and snatching up a pair of shorts. She pulls them up her legs and then adds a tank top, covering up her most delicious parts.

"That's not what we—"

"Don't you dare start spouting off rules to me," I snarl.

I stomp toward her and when her eyes widen, I stop. There isn't much space between us now, but it's still too much. I grip her forearms and tug her closer. She doesn't resist so I take that as a good sign.

"I'm done playing by your rules, Ruby. You've run this show for three years and I've played along. I'm done playing. I'm done being the nice guy, or more accurately, the fool."

She narrows her eyes, and I can't stop the tug of my lips at the crease in her forehead. I reach a hand up and smooth the wrinkle with the pad of my thumb.

"You've reached out for help and guess what? *I'm* the help. *I'm* the one you're going to have to deal with when it comes to whatever the hell is going on. *I'm* who you call when you need something from the club. *I'm* the person who will come, day or night, when you make that call." I shake her a little. "You hear me? I'm the one. Not my mom, not Sadie or Scarlett or Isaiah or anyone else. *Me*."

"Liam, I—"

"I'm not done."

I release her and she takes a few steps back and plops down to sit on the bed. I close the distance she created and stand at her knees. I tip her chin up with a finger, forcing her to look at me.

"Ruby, there's something here." I move my free hand between us. "You and me, we've got a connection. I have enjoyed the last three years, but I want more. I need more. I can't be your booty call and your protector. Not with your imposed rules. So, this is what's going to happen." I kneel in front of her. "Are you listening closely?" She nods. "You've got two choices."

"Okay."

"You can have the club's help and I'll coordinate everything, make sure you're safe from whatever it is you're afraid of. But I'll do it from a distance. Or," I pause for effect. "You can have all of me. But know this. If you choose all of me then that means *everything* changes. No more hiding your past. No more rules. No more secrets. I'm yours and you're mine."

11

RUBY

I'm yours and you're mine.

My eyes lock onto Liam's. Emotion swirls in the depths of his eyes, somehow matching the collision of fear and… hope in my soul. My earlier conversation with Isaiah mingles with Liam's words until I almost can't separate them.

After I filled Isaiah in on all of the ugly details of my time in the Army, of the recent resurfacing of my 'problem', I poured myself a few shots of Tequila and tried to numb my mind. I heard Liam knock on my door and wanted to ignore him. I should have known it wouldn't work. It never works. He's always there, in my apartment, in the bar, in my thoughts, in my fucking dreams. He's *always* there.

He's one of the good ones. Those were the last words Isaiah spoke to me before closing my apartment door behind him. He's one of the good ones and now that 'good one' is kneeling before me, giving me an ultimatum.

When I say nothing, Liam rises to his feet and his shoulders slump. "I guess I have my answer."

He turns and as I watch him walk away, something in me

shifts. I can't quite put a finger on what it is other than I don't like it. Not in the least.

"Wait," I call out as he reaches for the doorknob.

He freezes, arm outstretched, and glances over his shoulder.

"I don't want you to leave." I pull my lip in between my teeth.

Liam arches a brow but still doesn't turn completely around. "That isn't one of the options."

"Yes it is," I argue.

He finally faces me and shakes his head. "No, it isn't. Not wanting me to leave is not the same thing as wanting me to stay. As wanting me… all of me."

"Close enough."

He throws his arms up. "Dammit, Ruby! Why are you making this so fucking hard? I like you. More than I fucking should, apparently. And I think you like me. So, make a choice. All of me or none of me?"

I chew the inside of my cheek. It's not as easy as he makes it sound, this whole decision-making thing. Especially when it comes to my heart, my life. I decide to take a different approach because I don't know any other way to get him to understand my side of this. Not unless I want to tell him everything and I don't know if I'm ready for that.

"Can I show you something?"

He heaves a sigh and I know his patience is wearing thin. I just hope it lasts a few minutes longer. Long enough for him to agree.

"Well, can I?"

"Sure, what the hell?"

I give a nod and walk to the coffee table where my laptop is. I pick it up and sit on the couch, setting the computer on my lap. When a long moment passes and I'm still sitting alone, I look over at him and raise my brows.

Liam rolls his neck, then walks to the couch and sits next to me. I use my finger to roll over the trackpad, pointing the cursor where I want it to go. He sits there, quietly watching me, making my nerves jangle.

When what I want him to see is pulled up on the screen, I hand the laptop to him. "Here, read this."

Liam takes the device from me and leans forward with it in his large hands. I lean back against the couch while he reads the email from Eileen Dorsey. My heart races with each passing second. I close my eyes, squeezing them tight, so I don't have to see each time Liam tenses or the way his knuckles turn white as he grips the laptop with rage.

I don't know how much time passes but I feel the cushion shift when he leans back like I did. I can hear his breathing and it's ragged, infused with what I can only assume is anger. I just wish I felt confident that it's not aimed at me.

"Is what she says true?" he asks, his voice low and rumbling.

"Which part?"

I flinch when something touches my knee, and my eyes fly open in time to see Liam yanking his hand back. He seems to think better of it though and stretches it around my shoulders to pull me into his side. Air flutters past my lips and I allow myself to curl into him, to accept what he's offering.

"Ruby, I'm gonna need an answer?"

"To which question?" I counter, knowing he's waiting on a response to a couple.

"For starters, my last one." He rubs my shoulder with his thumb and the sensation is calming. "Is what Eileen wrote true?"

I swallow past the lump in my throat and answer very simply, "Yes."

His arm tightens slightly and rather than feeling confined,

I nudge into his side more. I know Liam thinks that I only want him around for the sex and honestly, that's part of it. The control that I've felt these last three years has been exactly what I needed but lately, it hasn't been enough for me either. I do want more with him. I want to let him past my defenses but to do that, I need to take him to my past and that's terrifying for me.

"Now it's my turn to ask," he starts. "Which part is true?"

My muscles stiffen but I concentrate on Liam's body heat, on the movement of his thumb, on his scent as it surrounds me. "All of it."

"Oh."

Liam and I sit there in silence, me wondering what the hell 'oh' means and him… well, I have no idea what he's thinking. That's the problem. When the silence becomes deafening, I pull away from him and scoot to the edge of the couch to brace my elbows on my knees.

"Oh? That's it? Just 'oh'?"

"I'm sorry, Ruby." He sighs and straightens next to me. "I'm trying to process what I read."

My stomach drops and irrationality takes over. "Does it change anything?" I ask, hoping beyond all hope that it doesn't.

Somehow, Liam seems to sense that my question refers to his earlier ultimatum. He cups my cheeks in his palms. "Not a damn thing."

Instant relief floods my system followed by a swift intake of breath. "Wait… so are you still giving me an ultimatum?"

Liam chuckles but it is without humor. "Is that how you took that?"

"Well, yeah."

"Then, yes, I'm still giving you an ultimatum."

"Okay."

Liam leans in and presses his lips to mine for a brief kiss.

A moan escapes me as he pulls back. “Do you have an answer?” he asks.

I stare into his eyes and nod.

“So what is it?”

I nod again, not trusting myself to speak.

Liam arches a brow and growls, “All of me?”

I open my mouth several times, but the words won’t come. Rather than nodding again, I answer him the only way I know how. I lunge forward and claim his lips with my own, thrusting my tongue past the seam to tangle with his.

12

LIAM

Ruby tastes like an intoxicating mix of Tequila and sin. Alarm bells war with fireworks in my brain, even as I pull her tank top off, unhook her bra and slide the straps down her arms. For an agonizing minute, the alarm bells win, and I lean back to look at her.

"Please tell me this means what I think it means," I plead.

Ruby's lips quirk up and that's all I need from her to shut the blaring sirens off for good. I yank her forward until she collides into my chest and she works her legs to straddle my hips.

My cock strains against my jeans and I want to free myself, but I don't want to break our connection, not again. Not now that I know what it means. Ruby grinds against me, increasing the pain in the most pleasurable way.

I nip at her bottom lip and suck it into my mouth, running my tongue along its plumpness. Ruby moans and I inhale the sound as if my life depends on it. Maybe it does.

"I need more," she groans.

Without breaking contact, I shake my head. I want to fuck her more than I want my next breath but that's not what

I came here for. And while the alarm bells have silenced, there's still the voice in the back of my head reminding me what I read in that email.

"Please," she pouts into my mouth.

I wrap my fingers around her shoulders and back away, staring into her eyes the entire time.

"Are you sure? Because this isn't why I came up—" She places a finger against my lips to silence me, but I gently pull it away. "I'm not leaving afterward," I warn her.

"Okay."

We stare at each other a moment longer before a growl crawls up my throat and I stand up with her in my arms. I carry her to the bed and throw her down. I brace myself on my arms on either side of her head and lean over her.

"No more rules."

"Okay."

"I take that back." Ruby's eyes grow round, and I smile to soften her fear. "One rule."

"Wh-what's that?"

"If I ever do something that triggers you or causes you to be afraid, you'll talk to me about it rather than shutting me out. I'll never hurt you and I'll always stop if you want me to stop. I know that no means no. But I need to know that you're in this as much as I am and that means communicating, no matter how uncomfortable or scary."

"That's a really long rule."

"I guess it is. But it's the one dealbreaker for me. I meant it when I said if you choose me, you choose all of me and that goes both ways. I want you but only if I can have all of you. The good, the bad, the infuriating and everything in your past."

My breath catches in my throat when she seems to have to think about it. It rushes past my lips when she lightly kisses me.

"I'm in."

"Yeah?" I ask too afraid for this to be all some sort of sick dream.

She nods. "Yep. I can't promise that I'll never be scared or that some things won't be hard for me, but I'll try. I like you, Liam. A lot."

"I like you too."

"I've got a lot of shit in my head, a lot of shit coming my way. I like the idea of having you by my side for it. I like that I'm not alone, despite all of my efforts to stay that way."

I let my weight settle on top of her and fuse my lips to hers. When her tongue pokes out, I nip at it. Ruby reaches between us and pops the snap on my jeans and tugs the zipper down. Her hand slides into my boxer briefs and she wraps her fingers around my throbbing dick.

I straighten and yank my shirt off, tossing it to the floor. I shuck the rest of my clothes and they join my shirt. By the time I'm done, Ruby has stripped off her shorts and panties as well. I let my gaze roam over her body, her perfect skin, all of her.

Ruby trails her fingertips over my chest, sending shivers down my spine. When she cups my balls and rolls them in her hands, I get lost in her touch. My body is screaming at me to take her, fuck her into oblivion so I'm the only man she ever thinks about but my heart reminds me to take it slow, show her that I can respect her demons while also making her forget them.

I wrap my fingers around her wrist and pull her hand away. Rather than take from her, I rub her clit with my thumb while sliding a finger into her wet pussy. Her hips buck wildly as her body begs for the release I'm not ready to give it.

I lean over her and whisper in her ear. "Shhh... just feel."

Ruby's moans intensify so I capture her lips in mine to

quiet her. It does little good, but I don't care. The way she tastes, the way she feels, the way she sounds... I'm here for it all.

"Li-Liam," she huffs into my mouth on a breathy moan. "Inside. I need..." She throws her head back when I speed up the circles I'm tracing around her clit, teasing and tantalizing.

"What do you need?"

"You. I need you," she pushes out.

I remove my hand from between our bodies and replace my finger with my cock, gliding into her easily. When I'm balls deep, I still my movements so I don't lose myself like some randy first timer. Ruby's nails dig into my chest, silently urging me to keep going. I allow myself to slowly pull out until just the tip is penetrating and when she curls her fingers and I feel the bite of her nails again, I slam into her, scooting her up the bed as I do.

"So fucking good," I groan. I grip the sheets in my hands at either side of her head and fuck her like my very existence depends on it.

Ruby lifts her hips in perfect rhythm with my thrusts. Sweat coats my body but I don't care. All I want, all I'm focused on is making this the best she's ever had and making sure she knows that I'm the only man in this room with her. I'm the only man that matters... in this moment and every moment after.

Jolts of electricity shoot down my spine and my hips want to lock up and surrender to the pleasure, but I'm not ready. Not yet. I balance my weight on one arm and, without slowing down, I use my free hand to urge her legs around my waist to grant me easier access to her ass.

I wet my finger in my mouth and reach around to her puckered hole, slowly circling it. Ruby reflexively tenses up but the noises coming from her assure me that she's okay with what I'm doing.

"Relax," I coax. "Breathe and relax, Ruby love."

I shove a finger inside and swirl it around, eliciting sounds from her that I've never heard. Guttural groans that only a woman on the brink of flying in ecstasy make. It takes a few moments to get the rhythm between my hips and my finger in sync but when I do, Ruby lets go and flies.

"Oooh, fuck!"

My spine stiffens as her pussy spasms around my cock, milking me for everything I've got. My arm starts to shake, and I worry that I won't be able to hold my weight off of her much longer, but I refuse to stop before she's able to ride this out as long as possible.

My orgasm ends but hers continues. And continues and continues. I remove my finger so I've got both arms to keep me upright and her moans begin to quiet, her body begins to slow. When she goes limp, I know she's satisfied.

I press a kiss to her lips before wrapping her in my arms and rolling to the side, taking her with me. She curls into my chest, her damp skin feeling fevered. I hold her close as I stare at the ceiling. The only sound around us is our labored breathing and a steady beat of music coming from the bar beneath us.

Ruby breaks the silence first. "That was…"

She runs her fingers over my chest and goosebumps break out over my flesh. When she doesn't finish her sentence, I can't help the nagging thoughts that plague me.

"That was what?" I ask, a touch of insecurity in my voice.

Ruby takes a deep breath and releases it quickly, cooling my body even more. "Different. That was different."

I tense up and when she rises up on her elbow, I know she felt it.

"Good 'different' or bad 'different'?"

"Amazing 'different'."

I roll my neck and when I see the smile on her face, the tension eases. I brush a wisp of damp hair out of her face and cup her cheek. My mind races with one thing and one thing only and I know I can't stop it from coming out of my mouth, no matter how hard I try.

"I love you, Ruby."

She blinks several times but says nothing. Her smile remains and I take that as a good sign.

"I don't want to scare you off, but you need to know that. Especially now that you said you're all—"

Ruby places a finger against my lips.

"I know, Liam," she says softly. She climbs on top of me to straddle my hips and places both hands on my cheeks.

"I'm not scared."

13

RUBY

Weird.

Different.

So damn good.

As I sit on the couch, my laptop balanced on my knees, I stare at Liam, still asleep in my bed. This is the first time he's been here when I woke up and it's weird. Or it was. Being the only one awake for two hours has given me time to process the fact that, in three years, I've never allowed him to stay after we fucked. While I know the reasons behind my demands of him, I'm beginning to see that they were probably pointless.

I tried to protect myself, and him, by keeping him at arm's length. I wanted nothing more than to have that human connection but on my terms. My crazy, ridiculous, *pointless* terms. Somehow, despite my walls, despite my rules, Liam snuck in. My fears haven't disappeared, and I still don't know if what's between us is the forever kind of thing, but I want it. I want him.

I meant what I said to him. The fact that he loves me doesn't scare me. I'm falling for Liam. Hard. He wasn't the first person I called when my world was rocked, but he was the first person I *wanted* to call and that means something.

"Morning."

Liam's voice pulls me from my thoughts, and I blink several times to bring his face back into focus. I lean forward to set my laptop on the table and toss the blanket wrapped around my shoulders to the side.

"What're you doing?" he asks as he swings his legs over the edge of the bed and stands.

My mouth dries up and my lungs seize as my gaze involuntarily lowers to take in his impressive morning erection. How am I supposed to answer a question when I can't even remember to breathe?

"Ruby?" He walks toward me, his cock my sole focus. Liam's fingers touch my chin and urge my head up. "Did you hear a word I said?"

"Uh..." I shake my head when words become impossible. Damn, he'd make a nun sin and praise the lord while she did it.

"You're adorable when you're distracted."

Liam drops a kiss on my forehead before heading to the kitchen and pouring himself a cup of coffee. The view of him walking away is just as impressive and I find myself still tongue tied.

"Am I imagining things, or did you tell me that you're not afraid of me loving you?" He quirks a brow as he takes a sip of coffee.

Apparently the 'L' word is enough to snap me out of my trance. "No," I say.

He carries his mug with him and sits next to me on the couch. "No what?"

"No, you aren't imagining things."

"Good to know." He drains his mug and sets it on the table before putting an arm around my shoulders and pulling me into his side. "So, what are you doing there?" He nods toward my laptop.

"Oh, um..." I lean forward and grab the computer to show him. "Just emailing Eileen back."

"You're gonna help her?" He scans the words on the screen.

"Yeah, I think so." I bite the inside of my cheek with uncertainty. I was sure of my decision when I typed the email but now that he's asking about it, I'm second guessing myself. "Unless you think that's a bad idea."

"Does it matter what I think?" The question may seem harsh to some but there's no heat to Liam's words. He genuinely wants to know.

I nod. "Of course."

"Okay." He puts the laptop on his other side and urges me onto his lap. I can't stop the rush of feeling in my core, despite there being nothing sexual in his demeanor. Liam frames my face in his hands and locks eyes with me. "If you want to help her, then I say go for it. If you want to keep your past and your experience to yourself, I'll support that too. I've got your back, no matter what you decide..."

His words trail off and my stomach flip-flops. "But?" I ask, certain there's more.

"But, if you decide to send that email and put yourself out there, I do have one request."

"What's that?"

"Let me be by your side the entire time. Let the club help in any way they can. Don't do it alone."

I think about what he's suggesting, about what it would mean to accept help. It's one thing to expose myself to danger but the club? All of them? Sure, I asked for their help but now that I've admitted my feelings for Liam, I've got mixed feelings about that decision. I'm not just hiring someone to protect me. I'm jeopardizing family.

You need them.

"I just don't want anyone to get hurt," I say. Liam isn't asking for an explanation, but I owe it to him. "You don't know Jensen, the power he has. There's no telling what he'll do if he's exposed for the predator that he is."

"Fuck Jensen." Liam's voice is laced with steel and there's a controlled fury beneath his calm exterior. "Do you really think that his rank or his threats scare me? Scare any of the Brotherhood?"

"That's just it," I argue. "You don't know him like I do. He single handedly ruined my military career. Hell, he ruined *me*."

"Aw, Ruby love, he didn't ruin you." Liam brushes a strand of hair out of my face.

"Yeah, Liam, he did. Our entire relationship up to this point is proof of that."

"Then tell me about him," he urges. "Let me carry some of that burden for you."

The sincerity in Liam's tone and the fact that I'm tired of the hold that Jensen has on me has me wanting to tell Liam everything. All the dirty details. And to do that, I have to go back to the beginning, to the day the course of my life was derailed.

I take a deep breath and hold it for a few seconds before blowing it out. I shift so that my back is pressed against his chest and his arms are wrapped around me. Somehow, not facing him makes this easier.

"For as long as I can remember, I wanted to join the Army. My parents weren't too thrilled." I let out a chuckle at the memory of all their attempts to change my mind. "In hindsight, I understand why they worried. I'm an only child, their little girl. They wanted me safe. But I wanted excitement. I wanted to serve my country the way my father did, the way Uncle Dusty did. And there was nothing they could say or do that was going to change my mind. So, I enlisted. I made it through boot camp and it was hard but it felt good, ya know? I survived something that a lot of people don't. Then I was sent to Fort Lee in Virginia for sixteen weeks of Advanced Individual Training."

"What was that for?"

"I've always had a knack for weapons and wanted to work toward being a small arms and artillery repairer. That required those additional sixteen weeks. Once I completed that, I was stationed at Fort Bliss and Sergeant Douglas Jensen was my commanding officer."

Liam's arms tighten around me, but it doesn't feel suffocating. It's comforting and exactly what I need.

"The first few days at Fort Bliss were fine, certainly better than the previous twenty-six weeks. It was mostly getting settled, all the check-ins with medical, housing, and every other department you can think of. And then it wasn't fine."

Ruby

Seven years ago...

"Banks!"

I bring my hand up to salute Sergeant Jensen. The very brief interactions I've had with him up to this point have told me nothing about the man other than he comes across as tough, but fair. This is my first time alone with the man and I want to show him that I've got what it takes to be a great soldier.

"At ease, Private."

I do as I'm told but I can't fully relax. Not with so much on the line. Not yet.

Jensen steps toward me, so close I can smell the coffee on his breath. He stares at my face for so long, I become uncomfortable and have to restrain myself from shuffling my feet under his scrutiny. When his eyes dip lower, heat surges in my cheeks and self-control becomes more difficult.

"Sir?"

Jensen continues his perusal of my body and ignores me. He circles around me twice, rubbing his chin as he does. I don't dare move a muscle because as uncomfortable as I am, I have no idea what he's doing. Maybe this is normal.

When he's facing me again, the grin on his face has my stomach bottoming out.

"You'll do, Banks." He's nodding while he's speaking. "You'll do."

I swallow past the lump in my throat. "Yes, sir. I'm excited for this opportunity and I won't let you down, sir. I know my way around weapons and—"

"Right… weapons."

"Yes, sir." Confusion swirls in my mind but I dismiss it as jitters. So the guy is weird. That doesn't mean anything.

"Private Banks, you're to report here Monday thru Friday at zero eight-hundred hours. For the most part, you'll be on your own. Private Jacks will handle your training the first few days and I'll do random inspections as I see fit. Any questions?"

So many.

"Yes, sir." I glance around the room at all of the equipment and weaponry. A zip of excitement rushes through my system knowing that I'll be working here, doing my part to serve my country and keeping other soldiers, and civilians, safe. "Where do I—"

Jensen glances at his watch and turns away from me, calling over his shoulder as he walks through the doorway. "Good luck, Banks. You're gonna need it."

Trepidation replaces my excitement but again, I dismiss it. No one ever said the military would be easy. I knew being young and female would work against me and maybe this is simply how that's playing out. Only time will tell.

Left alone, I have no idea where to start so I work my way through all of the weapons and familiarize myself with the workspace. I handle each piece of equipment and revel in the awesomeness that is surrounding me.

I did it. I joined the Army and am finally able to put my talents to good use. I'm so immersed in taking it all in that I don't even realize that eight hours have passed until my replacement arrives to take over.

It's another female Private and she's clearly not interested in small talk. She dismisses me before I can even learn her name and I shrug it off as nothing more than the focus required to do the job.

I spend the rest of the evening in the barracks and the rest of my first week goes smoothly. Jacks spends four hours each day training me, with the remainder of my shifts being used to implement what I learn. The following Monday, Jensen makes another appearance for what I assume is an inspection, cutting my training for the day short.

"Banks!" he hollers when he enters the room.

Both Jacks and I turn toward the door and stand at attention. Sergeant Jensen eyes us both and then focuses on Jacks.

"Take the rest of the day off, Jacks," Jensen instructs.

"Yes, sir."

Jacks walks to the door but before he exits, he glances over his shoulder and the look in his eyes is one I can't identify. Hesitation or pity maybe? Jensen never takes his gaze off of me, but he must sense that Jacks is hesitating and speaks again.

"Lock the door on your way out," he commands.

Jacks pauses a moment too long before saying, "Yes, sir."

Jacks mouths the words 'I'm sorry' and then does as he's told. A sense of foreboding skates over my body and I can't help but wonder what Jacks is sorry about. What does he know that I don't? Surely these inspections aren't that bad.

I'm so wrapped up in my own head that I don't realize Jensen has moved closer to me until his hand grazes my shoulder. I flinch at his touch, but it doesn't seem to bother him.

Before I can even process what's happening, Jensen smashes his mouth against mine and backs me up against a wall. I struggle against him and try to pound on his chest, push him away, anything to stop his assault. He's too strong, too rough.

This can't be happening. This can't be what my military career is going to be. This can't be the nightmare my dream is turning into.

When he's done, Jensen buttons his pants and straightens his uniform. He looks like nothing happened, like he didn't just shred my soul into tiny pieces.

"You better clean yourself up," he says, and his tone is so calm, so *normal*, that you'd never know he just raped some-one, raped me.

I glance around me to search for my clothes and realize that somehow, I'm on the floor about ten feet from the wall and I have no idea when or how I got here. I find my bra and panties and methodically put them on, all the while trying to keep him in my line of sight. Next is my uniform and boots.

When I'm fully clothed, it dawns on me that I'm surrounded by a damn arsenal and none of it could have helped me. These weapons aren't loaded. They aren't primed and ready to go. Every single thing in this room that should do me some good, can't.

"Get back to work, Banks," Jensen snaps. "You're behind schedule."

With that parting shot, he disappears down the hallway, the door slamming shut behind him. Somehow, I manage to get through the rest of my shift without completely falling apart. When my replacement arrives, she takes one look at me and that's when it hits me. She isn't focused on the job. She's broken. Jensen broke her and now he's moving on to fresh meat.

Jensen's reign of terror ends now. He's not going to do this to another woman. I won't let him. Scared, angry and determined, I don't go back to the barracks as I normally would. That won't do me or anyone else any good.

I go to the only place where I can get help: military police.

14

LIAM

Present day…

"They were no fucking help."

As Ruby recounts how everything with Jensen started, my muscles tense and anger boils my blood to the point I'm afraid I'll burn her simply by being near her. The police being no help, or being unable to help, isn't a new concept to me, especially growing up in the Broken Rebel Brotherhood, but I've accepted that not every law enforcement officer is like Jackson Stark.

I force my muscles to relax. "Did they do anything?"

"Oh, yeah, they did." Ruby's answer doesn't line up with the contempt in her voice but when she continues, I understand why. "They went straight to Jensen and asked him for his side of the story. Of course he denied everything. And because he was a respected sergeant, they believed him."

"What the fuck!?"

"That's how it is in the military. It's a good ol' boys club and anything that disrupts their carefully crafted reality is shoved to the side like it didn't happen or doesn't exist."

"That's bullshit," I snap, my control slipping.

"It is but what was I supposed to do? It was clear that it didn't matter what I said or if I reported anything. I never went back to the MPs again after that."

"What happened with Jensen after that report was made?"

Ruby pulls away from me and spins to face forward. She draws her knees into her chest, her toes hanging off the edge of the couch. I hate that she's still trying to carry the weight of it all on her own but she'll learn, in time, that she doesn't have to. I'm going to do whatever it takes to make sure she learns.

"He conducted his *inspections* once a month for the next three years." She spits the sentence out like it's poison sitting on her tongue. "Jensen made it very clear that I was a nobody in the Army and if I talked, I'd be labeled as crazy. Turns out, I didn't need to talk for that to happen."

"What do you mean?"

Ruby chuckles but there's nothing funny about it. "I was discharged from the Army because he broke me. My mind was so fractured, or at least, that's what he made people believe. I don't know anymore what was real and what was a manifestation of his lies. All I know for sure is that the Army thought I was nuts and that I could no longer perform my duties, so they sent me packing."

"You're not crazy, Ruby." I run my knuckle over her cheek, gently, reassuringly. "You're smart and beautiful and strong and opinionated and determined and every other positive thing I can think of. What you're absolutely *not*, is crazy."

She turns her head to look at me. "You really believe all that, don't you?"

"Yep."

"Even with all my rules and stipulations?"

I nod. "Here's the thing… now that I know the reason

behind them, they make sense. You were brutalized in the worst way possible, and all your quirks were just your way of protecting yourself, of maintaining control in a situation that you never had control of before. There's nothing wrong with that. But..."

"But what?"

"You don't need to protect yourself from me."

"I know."

"Do you?" I ask, needing her to be damn sure of me, especially knowing what I'm going to suggest.

"Yeah, Liam, I do. You've never once hurt me." She rolls her eyes. "Seriously, you're the most cooperative booty call ever."

"Had lots of booty calls, have you?" I tease.

Ruby instantly sobers. "No. I mean, I wasn't a saint when I joined the Army, but I didn't sleep around. I was eighteen and my parents were very protective of their little girl. Not much freedom to get into trouble."

"I never meant to suggest that you—"

She holds her hand up to stop me. "Don't. I know you were only teasing. And I really want you to understand something."

"What's that?"

"You're the only *man* I've been with. Sure, you're not my first, but you're the first that actually matters to me. Before Jensen... they were just puppy love. Special at the time but I knew they weren't the forever kind of special. And Jensen, well, was Jensen. You, Liam, are different. Better. *Important.*"

A warmth spreads through me at her words and I recognize it for what it is even if she doesn't say it in so many words: love. From the moment I got Dusty's letter I knew she would be different. Call it whatever you want, but I was doomed before I even met her. In the best possible way.

"Ditto."

A silence settles over the room but it's comfortable. I'm not waiting for her to throw me out or change her mind about us. I'm not expecting the other shoe to drop. I'm simply enjoying the moment and being with her.

Until she breaks the silence.

"So, now what?"

"We take things a day at a time."

"No." She shakes her head. "I mean, yes, I agree, but I wasn't talking about us. I was talking about Jensen. What do I do?"

"You mean what do *we* do?"

"Right."

"Well, I know it's not going to be easy, but I think we take it to the club. You've already taken the first step in requesting our help. Now they all need to know exactly what that means, what happened up until this point."

Ruby sighs and I hear the weight of it all in that one exhale. She's scared but I can't quite tell if it's for her or me or the club. The thing is, she's stronger than she thinks. And she has so many people who have her back.

"Should I send that email to Eileen?" she asks, glossing over my statement.

"That's up to you." I pick up her hand and squeeze it in mine. "But if you really want my advice..."

"I do, Liam. I need it."

"Then I would suggest waiting until after the club is fully informed and brought up to speed. I have a feeling that you agreeing to help is going to set a shit load of events into motion and I want to make sure we're all prepared before that happens."

"Yeah," she says while nodding. "Okay, that makes sense." She bites her lip nervously. "When do we talk with the club?"

"Today."

Her head whips up and she pins me with wide eyes. “Really? That soon?”

“The sooner we get the ball rolling, the sooner you can put it all behind you. Why wait?”

“Because I’m scared, that’s why!” she snaps, vehemence in her tone.

“I know you are, Ruby love. But you know what you’re not?”

“What?”

“Alone.”

15

RUBY

"I'm glad you decided to come and talk with everyone."

I fidget with my hands as I stand in front of Isaiah. I already told him my story, so he's not the one I'm worried about. I look around the room at the faces of club members, most of which I already know from the bar. My gaze lands on Liam and my stomach flips over. He's standing at the other end of a long table talking to Brie and Griffin, his parents, and Sadie and Micah. Liam must sense my stare because he turns his head and smiles.

"You told him everything?"

I refocus on Isaiah and there's concern etched into the lines of his forehead so I'm quick to respond. "Yeah."

"Based on that smile," he nods toward Liam, "I'd say it went well."

"As well as learning that information about your girlfriend can go."

"Girlfriend?" He raises his brows.

Heat creeps up my neck but is quickly replaced by a defensiveness that I can't stop. "Is that a problem?"

"No." Isaiah shakes his head. "I think it's great." After a long pause, he continues. "But as his best friend, and the president of this club, I need you to know that if you ever hurt him, it will destroy him. And if he's destroyed, this club is screwed. We need him. *I* need him."

"Look, Isaiah, I'm not going to stand here and make promises I don't even know if I can keep." I square my shoulders and look him straight in the eyes. "What I can promise is that I'll never hurt him intentionally. I..."

"You what?"

I lift a shoulder. "I'm falling in love with him."

"That's all I need to know." Isaiah looks over the room. "Okay, everyone, let's get things started." His demeanor switches from friendly to authoritative so quickly I find it hard to keep up. "Liam, the floor is yours today."

Everyone takes their seats and the air in the room thickens as they all focus on Liam, who has moved to stand next to me.

"I know today was supposed to be a day off for all of you, so I appreciate you getting here on such short notice." Liam drapes an arm around my shoulders. "For those of you who don't know, this is Ruby. She's the bartender at Dusty's." He pulls me into his side. "She's also mine so don't get any ideas."

"It's about time."

"Thank God."

"She's too good for you."

Based on the reactions of everyone around the table, I realize that I'm the only one who didn't see what was right in front of me. It's unsettling and at the same time, comforting.

"Welcome to the family," Brie says from the other end of the table.

My heart skips a beat at her statement, and I let out an awkward laugh. "You're getting a little ahead of yourself, Brie."

"You're with Liam." Griffin says the words like they explain everything.

"Yeah, but—"

"But nothing, honey," Griffin says. "You're with Liam and that makes you family."

Liam leans in close to my ear. "There's no point in arguing with them. Might as well accept your fate, smile and agree," he whispers.

I do what he says and realize that my agreement is sincere. The thought threw me for a loop, but I don't hate it. In fact, the more I think about it, the more natural it feels. I like being linked to Liam, to these people. They're good people.

"Now that we have that out of the way, let's get down to business." Liam's tone is brisk and almost businesslike. "I know that some of you are already aware that Ruby has requested our help and a few of you know why. I called today's meeting because it's time everyone is brought up to speed."

My stomach twists into an almost unbearable knot. There's no turning back now.

"I want to start by saying that I know all of you have military background and I don't. I also know that each and every one of you has a loyal streak a mile wide. But you're going to have to set that aside and keep an open mind with this case. It's going to test you in ways you haven't been tested before. Not only are we going to be going up against an actual person, who deserves whatever comes his way, but we're also gonna be fighting a much bigger enemy…" Liam pauses and scans the faces around the table. "… the US military."

Voices erupt and arguments ensue. I wish I could say the disbelief that's filling the space is a surprise but it's not. The military is a powerful force and one that produces the most loyal supporters. Being discharged from the military doesn't make a person any less, well, military. The saying 'once a marine, always a marine' is a saying for a reason.

Liam means well, but the dedication that the military breeds is hard for a civilian to understand, no matter how they were raised. It's not his fault but it will be his downfall if I don't start explaining. In an effort to gain everyone's attention, I do something I never thought I'd do again. I straighten my posture and salute.

It takes several moments before my stance is noticed but when it is, one by one each club member stands and salutes back. Liam's jaw drops but he quickly recovers. I relax my body and give a stiff nod to let them know they can too.

I speak over the sound of chairs scraping over the hardwood floor as they all sit back down. "I'm one of you," I begin. "I served our country in the Army because it's all I ever wanted to do. There was never a plan B in case it didn't work out. There wasn't any second-guessing or doubts about making the military my career. I certainly never thought I'd end up the jaded owner of a small-town bar with her lifelong dreams haunting her day in and day out. But here I am."

Each pair of eyes is glued to me and the longer I talk, the more comfortable I become. I take a deep breath and continue. "All I want, all Liam wants, is for you to hear me out. Listen to my story and if, when I'm done, you don't want to help, that's fine. I get—"

"It's not fucking 'fine'," Liam growls.

I rest a hand on his arm. "Yeah, Liam, it is." I glance at Isaiah, remembering that this is his club, his call. His face is grim, but he gives an almost imperceptible nod. "It's not my intention to destroy the institution but I do think things need to change, at least when it comes to sexual assault."

"Damn straight," Brie says vehemently.

"Why is this our fight?" Noah asks. "Can't we take care of the bad guy and call it good?"

"We could," Liam says. "But can you honestly sit there and say you'll be able to look yourself in the mirror if we do the bare minimum? We stop one asshole but there are ten more just like him."

Noah's protest dies and he leans back in his chair with his arms over his chest.

"'Help those who can't help themselves'." Isaiah speaks up. "That's the club's motto. That's what you took an oath to do when you joined. I'll back Ruby's wishes that there will be no questions asked if you decide not to take on this fight with us but don't for a second think that I'll agree with you if that's what you decide."

"We'll hear you out," Jace says.

"Ruby, why don't you start from the beginning?" Liam suggests before anyone else can voice their displeasure.

When Liam sits in the chair to the right of Isaiah, I clear my throat and start talking. I tell them about Jensen. I give them every last gory detail about the *inspections* he performed. The room is silent for the hour it takes me to tell my story, right up to the point where I was unceremoniously ditched by the Army. By the time I'm done, I can tell any uncertainty they've felt has disappeared. Angry, hardened eyes stare back at me. Determined veterans who have had their rose-colored glasses ripped off like an old band-aid.

"You said there are others," Isaiah prompts when I quit talking. "Tell us about that."

"I don't know for sure, but I got the impression that a few other female soldiers who served under Jensen had gone through the same thing I did." I shrug. "It's not like we all sat in a circle and talked about it. Jensen made sure of that. But in my gut, I know I wasn't the only one. And then there's Eileen Dorsey. She's the one who brought it all back up. She asked for my help, said there are others."

"How is this fucker still getting away with this?" Isabelle, Isaiah's twin, says from her chair.

"Not only is he getting away with it, but he's also advanced to Captain and being hailed as a damn hero for his service."

"Ruby, I don't mean to be insensitive, but you've been out for three years. What makes you so sure that he's going to cause trouble now?" This question is from Noah.

"Because I'm going to help Eileen and these other women," I respond. "Jensen made a lot of damn threats. The first he made was that he'd ruin my Army career and reputation. He did that."

"What other threats did he make?" Isaiah asks.

"In short, he will come after anyone who tries to take him down. As for me, if I talk, he'll kill me."

"He's not gonna fucking touch you," Liam barks.

"He'll try," I snap, my control slipping. I immediately regret my reaction. Rubbing my hands over my face, I heave a sigh. "I'm sorry, Liam. But you don't know him. He's not some thug off the street. He's got power and everything he needs at his fingertips to make my life a living hell. Even if he doesn't kill me, he won't rest until he's broken me again."

"That's where we come in," Isaiah says evenly. "Jensen might be some big hotshot in the Army, but we aren't a bunch of nobodies. We have connections, we have power, and more importantly, we have anger and determination fueling us. Fear is what will fuel Jensen. The fear of getting caught. The fear of his life being ruined. And people who operate under fear don't make smart decisions."

Isaiah turns to Liam. "VP, this is your show. How do you want to handle this?"

"To start, I want to add security at the bar. Two of us will be there every second the bar is open. I also want to put someone outside during off hours. Ruby lives above the bar and we aren't going to take any chances."

"You're not gonna be there?" Worry laces my tone, but I can't stop it from bleeding out.

"You're damn right I'm gonna be there," Liam assures me. "But I want that extra person, just in case." Relief washes over me. "I'll be with you for any encounter you have with anyone that's involved in this. If you meet with Eileen, I'll be there. If you meet with any attorneys or military personnel, I'll be there."

I expect anger to take over, but it doesn't. Instead, my relief intensifies. I don't want to do this alone. I want Liam next to me through all of it. I just hope I'm not jeopardizing his safety in the process.

"Have you already told Eileen that you'll help?" Isaiah asks.

"No, not yet. Liam thought it would be a good idea to get you guys up to speed first. I'll email her when I get home."

"I'm going to ask you to wait a few more days." Isaiah holds his hand up when Liam opens his mouth to protest. "Liam, think about it. We need to get a schedule in place for security and we need to dig up as much information on Jensen and the military's sexual assault policies and procedures."

"He's right," Micah says. As the former president and one of the founders of the club, when he talks, everyone listens. "We never go in blind. Liam, you're too close to this. I'm not suggesting that you can't handle it, but you have to treat it like Ruby's a client and not the woman you love."

"Because that's what you all did?" Liam counters through clenched teeth.

"That's enough," Isaiah demands. "Liam, this is your case." Isaiah cringes at the word and looks at me with apology. "But

Dad's right. You're too close. We do what we've always done. We prepare, we research, and then we fight."

"Two days. We've got two days to figure this shit out and that's it. I don't want this drug on any longer than it has to be. It's already taken too much from Ruby and I don't want it taking any more."

Liam steps close to me and puts his hand at the small of my back. It's a small gesture but there is so much feeling, meaning, emotion in that simple touch.

"Ruby, why don't you send Eileen an email and tell her you need a few days to think things over? That'll buy us time and hopefully she'll back off and give you a little breathing room. Does that work?"

"I can do that." I agree to do as Isaiah suggests but I'm with Liam on this. Now that everything's out in the open, I want this done and over. I want to take Jensen down and free these women from their living nightmare.

I want revenge. I want Jensen to pay for his crimes.

I want my damn life back.

16

LIAM

"Are you still mad at me?"

I look at my mom and register the sadness in her tone, in her expression. Ruby is outside with my dad, who's grilling up steaks for dinner. We'd been invited over after the club meeting adjourned and as much as I wanted to be alone with Ruby, I was equally happy to hang out with my family and see how Ruby handled herself with them.

"I was never mad at you."

"Bullshit." Mom chuckles. "You hated that I knew things about Ruby that you didn't. You have since the first time I met her. Which I'll remind you, you pushed for."

"I pushed for it because Dusty said it'd be good for her."

"I know."

"And I wasn't mad at you. I just hated the situation. I had no idea what she'd been through, but I knew it was bad. Dusty made that pretty clear in his letter."

"Still insisting on keeping that letter to yourself?"

I refused to show the letter to anyone. It seemed like a violation of trust somehow. I did what I was asked to do, and I brought Ruby together with the women of the club. I told them as much as they needed to know, which admittedly wasn't much. How could I tell them something I didn't know myself?

"The only other person who will ever see that letter is Ruby."

Mom pats me on the cheek. "You're a good man, Liam. Your dad and I must have done something right."

"Brie, baby, leave him alone." Dad steps through the patio door carrying a tray full of perfectly grilled meat, Ruby on his heels.

"I'll do no such thing, Griff. He's my son and I'll say anything I damn well please."

"What's going on?" Ruby asks, uncertainty dancing in her eyes.

"Nothing," I assure her as I let my dad pass and then I step closer to her. "Just telling my mom how great you are."

"What my son fails to recognize is that I already knew you were great." Mom winks at her and Ruby laughs self-consciously. "I'm just glad you finally figured out how awesome *he* is."

A blush stains Ruby's cheeks and I lean in to kiss them, one at a time, before settling my lips on hers for a brief peck.

When I pull back, the blush has darkened. In an effort to erase her unease, I change the subject. "I'm starving." I turn to face my parents. "Let's eat."

Conversation abandoned, we all take our seats and dig into the meal. While I fill my mouth and stomach, I watch Ruby. At first, she's tentative, taking small bites and being super polite. After a few minutes though, I can see her shoulders ease and her reservation lessen.

"Ruby, has Liam ever told you the story about when he was fifteen and threw a party out in one of the fields?" Dad asks.

Ruby swallows and wipes her mouth with the napkin. "No."

"Do we re—"

"Shit, I forgot about that." Mom howls with laughter. "Liam, Isaiah, and Isabelle thought it would be a good idea to throw a party while we were all on a job. Emersyn and Doc were still on the property, so we thought nothing about leaving the kids home. Little did we know that they were going to raid the bar at the main house and invite everybody they knew over."

"There weren't that many people," I insist, trying to recapture my dignity.

"Son, there were over sixty teenagers whose parents we had to call," Dad reminds me. "Not to mention Lila, who was even younger. At least she stayed away from the alcohol, if not all of the bad decisions. But you..." Dad points a finger in my direction. "You were the icing on the cake. You had to be carried inside and then you were only able to crawl to the bathroom to worship the porcelain god."

"Seriously?" Ruby asks with a glint in her eye.

"Then there was the time he brought a girl to the house and —"

"Okay, she doesn't need all the childhood stories tonight," I groan.

"Fine. What about you, Ruby?" Mom looks at her. "Tell us about your childhood."

"Not much to tell. My dad was in the Army, so we moved around a lot. I spent a lot of time with Uncle Dusty after he was discharged. I'm an only child so my parents were very over-protective. But really, they were great. I couldn't ask for better parents."

I clear my throat. "When was the last time you saw them?"

"It's been a while." A guilty look crosses her face, but she manages to mask it quickly. "I wasn't able to make it home for Uncle Dusty's funeral, but I'd seen them about a month before that when they came to visit."

"You haven't seen your parents in over five years?"

"It's not that I don't want to but..."

"But what?" Mom prompts when Ruby doesn't finish.

"Jensen threatened them. It just seemed safer to not let people I love near me."

I can't imagine not seeing my parents for that long. Even when I went to college, I was home a lot and not only because I needed my laundry done. My family is my world.

"Well, that needs to change," Mom says and then turns to me. "You should take her to see her family. Or invite them here. There's plenty of space at the main house or they can stay in our guest room. When things settle down, of course."

"There's also plenty of room at my place," I remind her. Ruby's never been to my house. We always hooked up at her apartment. The more I think about it, the more the idea of her in my living room, at my dining table, *in my bed* takes root. I look at Ruby. "Actually, you should probably stay at my place for a while."

"No." She shakes her head. "There will be plenty of security at my place."

"Yes, but you'll still be safer on BRB property," I argue.

"Maybe, but that's beside the point." She shifts her gaze to my parents and then back to me. "Maybe we can talk about this later?"

"Oh, honey, just pretend we're not here," Mom says as she props her chin on her palm and her elbow on the table, like she's settling in for a major gossip session.

"We're going to be together every night anyway. What does it matter whose place it is?"

"We only started dating, or whatever you want to call it, yesterday. I just don't want to move too fast."

"We've been seeing each other for three years."

"We've been... *really good friends* for three years. There's a difference." Ruby covers my hand with one of hers. "Liam, just because I don't want to move in with you doesn't mean we can't alternate between our two places. It also doesn't mean that I don't want to be with you."

She's right, of course, but it doesn't make it any easier to swallow.

"Son," Dad interrupts. "Take things one day at a time. The rest will come."

"For the record, your father is shit at taking his own advice." The smirk on my mom's face is all the evidence I need to know that, while she's being honest, my mom is messing with my dad. "You two need to do what works for you, not what we did or what anyone else tells you to do."

I know that Ruby is fully capable of digging in her feet if I try to argue with her. I also know that I don't want to do anything that could destroy what's between us, so I'll leave it alone. Besides, who wants to discuss their sex life in front of their parents?

"Fine," I agree grudgingly. "But there won't be a night that you're alone."

Ruby smiles and stabs at her food with her fork. "I'm good with that." She pops a bite of steak into her mouth and just like that, the conversation is over.

~

"Are you sure you're okay with this?"

I extend my hand to help Ruby off my Harley. She hesitantly takes it and swings her leg over the seat, staring at my cabin the entire time.

"This is where you live?" she asks.

I swing my gaze to take in what she's looking at and try to see it the way she does. I don't know what she expected but now I'm nervous that it was anything but what she's getting.

"Yeah." I rub my chin with my free hand. "It's just a starter home. A roof over my head until I can build exactly what I want or add on to it."

Ruby's eyes meet mine and she tilts her head. "Why are you doing that?"

"Doing what?"

"Trying to justify where you live?" I shift uncomfortably and she continues. "Liam, I live in a tiny ass apartment above a bar. This," she points to my house, "is a fucking mansion compared to that. I'd give anything to live in a place like this."

"We can make that happen." I'm only half joking. My suggestion earlier that she move in with me wasn't only because I worry about what will happen once she sends that email. I genuinely want her with me.

Ruby chuckles away my suggestion. "Take me inside."

"Yes, ma'am."

I lead her up the front steps and pause only long enough to unlock the door. When we step over the threshold, her sharp intake of breath reaches my ears. I watch as she lets her gaze roam over the open space.

I was honest with Ruby when I said that this is a 'starter home' but deep down, I'm hoping she loves it as much as I do and we can just add on someday. There are two bedrooms and two bathrooms, something I insisted on when it was built. The loft houses my office, where I've got multiple computers set up to handle the club's work. Oversized leather furniture fills the living room with a seventy-inch flatscreen above the fireplace. Okay, so maybe this isn't an ordinary starter home.

"Are we just going to stand here or are you going to give me a tour?" she asks.

"Right… a tour."

She can see most everything from where we stand but I go through the motions anyway. When we take the stairs up to the loft, she gasps at the monitors. This is the one space that doesn't have that log cabin feel, with all of the monitors and wires and tech gear.

"What do you need all of this for?"

It dawns on me that she doesn't really know what I do. I think back over conversations that we've had since the day we met and realize that my job, or what I do for the club, has never come up. Time to rectify that.

I place my hands on her shoulders and guide her to the executive leather chair that I use and urge her to sit. I brush my hands over the keyboard and type in my passwords to bring the screens to life.

"Holy shit," she breathes.

"I'm kind of a nerd." I shrug.

"Or a genius," she mumbles.

"Definitely not a genius. Unless we're talking about my abilities in the sack and then I'll happily agree with you."

Ruby smacks me in the stomach and we both laugh. When she sobers, she spins the chair so she's facing me.

"My earlier question stands. What do you need all of this for?"

"Research mostly. I do all of the background checks for the club, gather intel, hack into systems when we need to. My dad did all of this when the club was formed and I took over. Got my degrees in computer science and criminal justice."

"Wait... you have two degrees?"

I shove my hands in my pockets and rock back on my heels. This isn't something that I like to talk about. The Broken Rebel Brotherhood is a club for military veterans and I'm not that. I put my skills to use the only way I knew how but it doesn't change the fact that, at times, I feel like I'm a disappointment.

When I don't respond, Ruby's hand touches my forearm, and she smiles. "You know that your family is proud of you, right?"

My eyes widen at her perceptiveness. I've never talked to anyone about my self-doubt. In fact, I've done everything in my power to shove it down and ignore it.

"Do you remember the first time we met?" she asks, which throws me off guard because it seems like a complete subject change.

"Of course."

"I was a hot mess and there you were, a light in a very dark tunnel. Other than convenience store clerks, front-desk hotel staff and my parents during extremely brief phone calls, you were the first person I talked to when I was discharged." She leans back in the chair and smiles, remembering.

"You may not have served in the military. You may not know what it's like to go from military life to civilian life, but you have this innate ability to be exactly what a person needs, no matter what the situation."

"Doesn't chan—"

Ruby holds a hand up to stop my protest. "Let me finish." She takes a deep breath and slowly releases it. "You took one look at me and… I don't know, I felt like I didn't need to be someone I wasn't. I felt understood even though that should have been impossible because you knew nothing about me other than what Uncle Dusty told you. And then I met your mom and Sadie and the other women of the club…"

17

RUBY

Three years ago...

Y*ou can do this, Ruby girl.*

Uncle Dusty's voice rings in my head, despite him being dead. I stare at the bar through my dirty driver's side window and swallow back the bile that creeps up my throat. I'm exhausted and hungry and so damn broken that I fear I won't be able to carry out his wishes.

I shift in my seat to dig his letter out of my bag. When my fingers touch the paper, I pull it out and flip to the last page.

Liam is one of the good ones...

Those are the words that I've read over and over and over, the ones that have propelled me forward the last few days. If Uncle Dusty says he's one of the good ones, then maybe he is.

You'll never find out if you stay in your car.

I take a deep breath and look at the building again. A man is standing in the doorway and I can only assume, based on the way his arms are crossed over his chest and he's staring at my car, that he's Liam. He's leaning against the building like he hasn't a care in the world, but his tapping foot gives off a vibe of annoyance. My palms become sweaty, and I shove the letter in my bag before I ruin it.

I slip my hand through the strap on my bag and drag it across the center console as I open my door. My gaze never wavers from the man as I close the door behind me and close the distance between us. When I'm a few feet away, he drops his arms to his sides and stands straight.

Two things happen simultaneously: my mouth goes bone dry and the nerves twisting my insides into knots morphs into butterflies. If this is Liam, I'm fucked. He's over six feet of muscular sin and checks all my boxes as far as physical attraction goes. Too bad I'm damaged and in no position to act on it.

When the silence lingers, any trace of his annoyance disappears, and he thrusts his hand out. "You must be Ruby." A jolt of lightning races up my arm when I shake his hand and I resist the urge to yank it back. "I'm Liam. Welcome to Dusty's."

I can only nod because my tongue won't come unglued from the roof of my mouth. What is happening to me? I'm dead inside, as dead as my uncle is and he's six feet under.

Clearly, you're not dead if your reaction to this hunk is any indication.

I shake the thought from my head. "I'm Ruby," I force out.

Liam chuckles and says, "Yeah. We've established that."

"Oh." Fuck, I'm being an idiot. I haven't been this tongue-tied since John Ferns asked me to prom my junior year of high school. "Should we go inside?"

"Yeah." Liam tips his head toward my car. "Do you have bags to get or anything? I can run those upstairs first if you want."

I shake my head. "No, that's okay. I'll get them later. Let's just get this over with."

I immediately want to call back the words. Liam is here because my uncle asked him to be. He could've said 'fuck it' and let the bar crash and burn in Dusty's absence but he hasn't. He's sent me regular emails, updating me on the bar. I never respond but my lack of participation doesn't seem to have deterred him.

You're going to deter him now if you don't get your shit together.

"Sorry." I square my shoulders in an effort to regain my composure. "I'm exhausted but I didn't mean to take it out on you."

Liam's eyes soften and he flashes a smile. "No need to apologize." He turns and opens the door, sweeping his arm to the side. "After you."

I take a deep breath and step across the threshold. I glance around the bar, taking in the few customers and sparse decor. It's easy to see why Uncle Dusty loved this place but it needs an overhaul. At the very least, some updating.

"We can go back to the office or sit at the bar." He touches the small of my back and I flinch. Rather than remove his hand, he flattens it and urges me forward. "C'mon, let's go to the office."

I let him guide me through the tables and try not to get impatient when he stops to introduce me to the customers. I know I should be grateful that Liam's here at all but I'm already on edge and need to take things one step at a time. I say none of this of course and instead, paste a smile on my face and let him make his introductions.

After Liam introduces me to Cindy, he walks me through a swinging door and the kitchen to a small office in the back of the building. I look to my left and then my right, my gaze landing on a folded chair against the wall. I go to grab it and he rests his hand on my arm.

"This is your office, Ruby." He nods toward the worn looking desk chair. "Take your place at the helm and I'll sit on this."

Liam snags the folding chair and sets it in front of the ancient metal desk. When he sits down, he remains silent but watchful. It takes me several moments to accept that what he said is true but when I do, it's like a switch flips. I drop my duffel next to the wall and take my place in my uncle's chair.

I run my hands over the desk and close my eyes, wishing that somehow, I could feel my uncle's presence. When it doesn't happen, I open my eyes and am met with a piercing green gaze, the kind that makes a person feel like their soul is being analyzed.

I clear my throat. "So, what should we discuss first?"

"That's up to you."

"Oh." Tension fills the room and based on the grin Liam's sporting, I'm pretty sure I'm the only one feeling it.

"Why don't you tell me a little bit about yourself?" he suggests.

Fuck. Of course he'd suggest the one thing I'm not prepared to do.

"Not much to tell." I shrug as if that's the truth. "I was in the Army and now I'm not. Dusty was my uncle and left this place to me, which you already know." I pretend I'm thinking of more to say when in reality, I already know that's all the information he's going to get out of me. "Oh, and I have no clue how to run a bar."

Liam laughs and somehow, that eases the tension in my muscles. "Something tells me that there is so much more to you than that, but I'll let it go for now. Just know that I'm here if you wanna talk." He snaps his fingers as if a thought just occurred to him. "You can also talk with my mom and her friends. Dusty wanted me to introduce you to them but I doubt I'll be given a chance. They'll be here to introduce themselves within twenty-four hours." He must sense my alarm because he winks. "I'll hold them off as long as I can."

"That would be…" What? Great, nice, appreciated? I shake my head. "Thank you."

"No problem. I'm here to make this as easy for you as possible."

Again, silence surrounds us but it's a little less uncomfortable. I don't know what it is about this man but he's making this as painless as possible and for that, I'm grateful.

"Let's start with the books," he says and reaches for a laptop on the desk. Turning it to face him, he types for a few seconds before turning it back toward me. "Do you mind if I come around next to you? It'll be easier to go over this stuff that way."

And have him be that much closer? I'm not sure I'm ready for that, which makes my next suggestion that much more ludicrous, but it doesn't stop me.

"Why don't you show me the apartment and we can talk up there?" In my mind, I see myself being able to put more distance between us with an entire apartment versus a small office.

Liam's eyes widen but only for a split second. He rises from his chair and folds it to put it back where it was. When he picks up my duffel bag and slings it over his shoulder, his muscles bunch beneath his T-shirt. I begin to see the failed logic in my suggestion but there's no turning back now, not if I want to seem normal.

"Can you grab the laptop and those folders?" He tips his head to indicate what is on the desk. "It has everything we'll need."

"Sure."

I grab the items and follow him out of the office and

around the corner to a set of stairs. He steps aside to let me go first and I can't help but wonder if he's looking at my ass on the way up.

"Should be unlocked," he says from behind me. "I tried to make sure you had the essentials in the fridge, so I was up here this morning. I hope that's okay."

"That's fine."

When I step inside my new home, my knees begin to shake and my hand flies to my mouth. Turns out, *this* is where I feel Uncle Dusty's presence and it's almost more than I can take.

"Are you okay?"

Tears burn the back of my eyes and when one spills over, I'm powerless to stop the ones that follow. Sobs wrack my body and when my knees buckle, I'm surprised to feel Liam's arms catch me. He carries me to the couch and sets me down. He sits next to me and wraps his arm around my shoulders, pulling me close.

"Shhh," he croons. "It's okay, Ruby. Let it out."

And that's exactly what I do. I let out all of the pain, all of the heartache that's built up over the years. I cry for the man that knew me so well, yet never pushed when he sensed I was struggling. I grieve an uncle that I'll never see again yet will see every day for the rest of my life, as long as I'm in this place. I sob for the girl I was and the woman I've become. I bleed tears for a life that I'll never have.

And all the while, Liam is there. Comforting, calm, rock fucking steady. When my crying subsides, I realize that he's rubbing circles over my shoulder and the motion is not only soothing, it's intoxicating.

"Feel better?"

I look up at him from beneath wet lashes and lust hits me fast and hard. I know that this is the last man I should be seeking a connection with, but he feels safe. And I desperately need to feel something good and safe.

I sit up a little and flatten my palms against his chest. It's been so long since I initiated anything with a man, and I hope I don't fuck it up.

"Kiss me?"

"Ruby, are you—"

"No talking," I whisper, inches from his lips. "Liam, I just… I need this. Please?"

I know I sound pathetic and there's a part of me that hates it but the bigger part of me recognizes it for what it is. Something good in an otherwise shit world. Something I can control.

Liam's gaze drops to my mouth and I lick my lips, craving him more than anything else. He lets out a ragged breath and mumbles, "Heaven help me."

18

LIAM

Present day...

Hearing Ruby recount the day we met is almost painful. I was so annoyed about her lack of communication before she said she was coming but it disappeared when I stood there and watched her struggle to get out of her car. I knew, based on Dusty's letter, that she was going to have baggage, but I didn't realize how vulnerable she really was. Sure, I sensed it at the time, but it's different hearing what it was like from her point of view.

"Anyway," she flaps her hand dismissively. "You know what happened next."

I smile. "Hard to forget." I remember how this little recap started and remind her. "You mentioned when you met my mom and the others."

"Oh yeah… that." She chuckles. "Damn, it was humiliating."

"Why?"

"You don't remember?" I shake my head, trying to summon

the memory and coming up blank. "We went back downstairs after we... well, after, and there they were, lined up at the bar. I didn't know who they were and when you introduced them, I wanted to crawl into my skin and never come out."

A lightbulb flashes in my head. "Holy shit, I'd forgotten about that. I must have been too pussy drunk."

"After you introduced us, you told me you'd be back the next day to discuss the bar and then you left. I had to sit there and talk to the mother of the guy I just fucked like it hadn't happened. But she knew. I know she knew."

"She couldn't have known," I insist.

"You didn't see the looks she was giving me. She was sizing me up, trying to figure out who the trollop was who slept with her son."

"You're not a trollop."

"Maybe." She sighs. "It doesn't matter now. She may have been sizing me up, but she still had this way about her. All of them did. They talked to me about the club, told me what you guys do. It wasn't long before I forgot that I didn't want anyone to know what happened to me and spilled my guts. I instinctively knew I could trust them."

"I still can't believe my mom has known your secret this entire time and you wouldn't tell me."

"Liam, you have to understand something. At the time, I was so fucking broken. I felt safe with you though and a lot of that was *because* you didn't know what had happened. And because of you, because of the space you gave me, the control you let me have, I'm a little less broken."

I cup her cheek. "Ruby love, I'm glad I helped. And I will do everything I can to keep helping, to keep breaking down your walls, but you need to know something."

"What's that?"

"I never thought you were broken. I hate that that's how

you see yourself, but I suppose I get it. But I never saw you that way and I never will."

"See, this is what I mean. You always know what to say or do. And that day, the day we met and I met your mom? She said something to me that I'll never forget."

"I'm almost afraid to ask, but what did she say?"

"She said that she understood my fear, understood what I'd been through, and that you would too. She said you're one of the good ones. I know she's your mom and some people might say that she had to say that, but the truth is, she didn't. Not every parent would hear my story and still be okay with their son being in my life. She loves you and so does your dad. They're proud of the man you are."

I let her words sink in. "Thank you."

"For what?"

"For helping me to see that. I've always felt, I don't know, a little like I'm the black sheep of the club, but it's nice to know that no one else sees me that way."

"It can't have been easy being surrounded by people who the world sees as heroes because of their military service but Liam? Being in the military doesn't automatically make someone a hero. Hell, look at Jensen. He's the furthest thing from one. As far as I'm concerned, being kind, being supportive, being present and understanding… those are the things that make a person a hero. You may not be the world's hero, but you're mine."

"You're certainly good for a man's ego."

I try to dismiss her words, deny them because they make me uncomfortable, but Ruby is having none of that.

"Don't," she snaps. "Don't dismiss what I'm saying. Don't dismiss how you've helped me. And so many others through the club. You want me to see myself in the same light that you see me in and all I'm doing is the same. I want you to see you the way I do." She pauses and takes a deep breath. "You've never been a hypocrite so don't start now."

"Point taken."

"Good." Ruby stands from the chair and rests her hands on my waist. "Now, does the tour stop here, in your office, or are you gonna show me your bedroom?"

Her fingers make their way to the fly of my jeans and she drags it down before sliding her hand into my boxer briefs. She grips my cock and pumps it a few times until a groan crawls up my throat. I wrap my hands around her wrists and pull, freeing myself so I can lift her up.

Ruby locks her ankles at my back and I turn to back her against a wall, slamming my mouth over hers as I do. She threads her fingers through my hair and kisses me with an intensity that rivals my own. Fucking her is the only way this ends but there's no time to get naked. I shove my jeans and boxers down over my hips, letting them stop around my thighs.

"Straighten your legs," I command.

She does but I hold her up so her feet don't touch the floor. I unbutton her jeans and push them down until they pool at her ankles. She kicks them completely off and brings her legs around me again.

With a hard, smooth thrust, I impale her. Her mouth drops open on a moan and her eyes roll back.

"Look at me," I growl, fucking her hard and fast.

When her eyes meet mine, her pupils dilate and her breathing becomes choppy. Need rages from within. The need to possess her, the need to claim her, the need to love her.

My spine tingles and I know I'm close. Too close. I reach between our bodies and press my thumb against her clit.

"Come for me, Ruby love," I grit out from between clenched teeth.

Her pussy clamps down and my dick throbs in her silky wet heat, both of us exploding. When we're sated and my hips slow, I lean my forehead against hers.

On a ragged breath I say, "I'll show you the bedroom now."

19

RUBY

"Can I get another beer?"

I stop wiping down the bar and glance at the man who just walked up and set his empty bottle down. Liam is at a table with a few other club members, but I feel his gaze on me. I don't recognize this customer as one of my regulars. Hell, I don't even recognize him as someone who belongs here, and Liam must sense it too because he hasn't stopped watching him since he came in.

"Sure." I offer a smile and turn my back to grab a Miller High Life from the cooler. When I hand it to him, his fingers brush mine and I make a conscious effort not to recoil. "Can I get you anything else?"

He tilts his head and stares, as if sizing me up, and then he shakes his head. "Unless you want to give me your number, no."

A nervous chuckle escapes me. "I'm taken." I nod toward Liam and the guy's head swivels. "Pretty sure he'd be upset if I gave my number out."

"Ah, right." He rasps his knuckles on the bar. "Can't blame a guy for trying."

He tosses a fifty down on the bartop, which is more than enough to pay for his two beers and a generous tip. I make change in the register, pocketing my cut, and when I turn back around, I see him set his full bottle on a table close to the door and walk out.

Huh? Odd.

Putting the clean-cut stranger out of my mind, I make my rounds to see if any of the customers need a refill. By the time I'm done, Liam is behind the bar and he's talking to a female customer as he serves her what looks like a vodka tonic.

The woman has shoulder length brown hair and when I make it to Liam's side and see her face, I notice that she doesn't look old enough to drive, let alone drink. I appreciate Liam's help but if he gets me shut down, I'm gonna be pissed.

"Did you check her ID?" I whisper when she takes her drink and makes her way to the table.

Liam's face sobers. "I did." He rubs the back of his neck and then crosses his arms over his chest. "Today is her twenty-first birthday."

"Okay." I drag the word out, not sure why that is something that has him in such a focused state. "What's wrong?"

Liam twists his head to look at the woman and then returns his attention back to me, his brow furrowed. "Her name is Eileen Dorsey."

Shock settles like sand in my stomach. He could have told me she was Mrs. Claus and I wouldn't have been more surprised. I brace myself against the counter and try to suck in air. My lungs don't seem to want to work and it's only seconds before the room starts to spin and my knees wobble.

"Hey, hey." Liam's hand rests on my back. "You need to breathe, Ruby love. Close your eyes and focus on my touch." He rubs circles between my shoulder blades, never slowing. I try to quiet my mind and only let *him* in. Finally, breathing comes easier. "There ya go. That's better."

I turn into him and let him wrap his arm around my shoulders to guide me back through the kitchen to the office. He presses me down into my chair and places a kiss on the top of my head.

"Be right back."

Before I can respond, he leaves me alone with my questions. Why is she here? Did something happen? She's so damn young. Will Jensen track her here? My thoughts whirl out of control, rattle around in my brain like laundry stuck on the spin cycle.

I startle when Liam walks back in and closes the door behind him. "Cindy's handling the bar and Isabelle, Tillie and Lila are helping. The guys are also outside, keeping an eye out in case she was followed."

I breathe a sigh of relief that at least one of my concerns is being addressed. If Eileen was followed, they won't get inside, get to me. Not tonight anyway.

"Thank you."

"You're welcome." He steps around the desk and leans against it, stretching his legs out and crossing them at the ankles.

"Why would she come here?" I ask.

"I don't know, Ruby love. But she's here and I don't think we can ignore that."

"Of course not," I snap. I may not be one hundred percent ready to deal with any of this but I'm not going to turn her away. Especially not now that I know how young she is.

"She's no younger than you were."

Liam's voice is quiet, almost hushed, but his words make me realize I'd been voicing my thoughts out loud.

"Look," he begins when I remain silent. "Her age isn't relevant unless we're talking about the legal drinking age because we're in a bar. As far as what she's going through, what you went through, age doesn't fucking matter. It's horrific no matter what."

He's right, of course, but I can't get the number out of my head. Maybe it's because she looks much younger than she is or maybe it's because, at her age, I'd already been dealing with Jensen for what felt like a lifetime. How long has she endured his vileness before speaking up?

When I find my voice again, I ask, "What do we do now?"

"That's up to you." He makes it sound like we're talking about whether or not to go to the store for milk now or later. He makes it sound simple when it's not simple at all. "You're certainly within your rights to ask her to leave if she's making you too uncomfortable. Or we could see if she wants to come back here and talk, away from the gossip-hive bar customers tend to be."

"We?"

Liam pushes off the desk and kneels down in front of me. He lifts my hands in his and squeezes. "Yeah, Ruby, we. You're not alone anymore. I'm here and I've got your back. The club has your back. You never have to face any of this on your own again."

I nod. "Okay. Thanks."

"You'd do the same for me."

I consider that and realize he's right. I would. I'd go to the ends of the Earth to do the same for him. I'd stand up for him, have his back, kill a motherfucker if Liam was hurt.

Why then, can't you do the same for yourself?

Well, shit. Put in those terms, I don't have an answer. Because that's exactly who Eileen is. She is me and I am her. We may have unique DNA, unique bodies, but we're essentially the same person. We have the same awful experiences, the same dreams, the same nightmares, the same fear and hopelessness and the same questions about our sanity. I couldn't save myself, not at the time, but maybe I can save her, save the unknown number of other women just like us.

Mind made up, I rise from my chair and square my shoulders. I take a few deep breaths and watch as Liam stands. We lock eyes and I can tell the precise second he knows what I'm thinking because he grins and gives a quick nod.

"I'll go ask her to come back." I grasp his arm when he turns to go do just that and he arches a brow in question. "What is it?"

"I've got this."

I step around Liam and walk through the kitchen and the swinging doors. I stop when I spot Eileen at the same table, her glass empty. She's looking around the room, probably trying to find me, and I recognize the emotion etched in her expression: resignation.

I make my way to her with determination, with a purpose. I sit down in the booth across from her and her eyes widen briefly before I notice the sheen in them that tells me she's perilously close to crying.

"Eileen?" I reach my hand across the table and she takes it. Her palm is clammy and she's shaking. "It's going to be okay."

I have no idea if that's true or not, but I wish someone had cared enough to say that to me. I give her a few minutes to pull herself together, knowing that she needs that. She needs to move past the hurt, the pain, and full throttle it straight into fucking pissed. Anger is what will get her through this. Anger and support.

"I'm sorry," she mumbles after several minutes.

"You don't have to apologize to me," I assure her.

"Yeah, I do," she insists. "I told you I'd give you time to figure out what you wanted to do and then I just showed up here. I know I should've waited but after last night, I couldn't."

The fine hairs on the back of my neck stand at attention. "What happened last night?"

She drops her gaze and fidgets with her glass, rolling it back and forth between her hands. "I have a little sister, Erin, and she, um…" She lifts the glass and seems to stare through it. "Can I get another one of these?"

Before I can get up, Liam is there, fresh drink in hand. "Here." He sets it in front of her and then sits down next to me.

Eileen spares him a glance before gulping down her drink. "Thanks."

"No problem."

Eileen looks back and forth between me and Liam. "Is he—"

"He's my…" I get tripped up on the word 'boyfriend' and can only hope Liam isn't upset by it. "This is Liam. He knows everything so you can talk freely."

"Oh." She frowns. "I thought he was the bartender."

"I'm whatever Ruby needs me to be," Liam says.

"Eileen, what happened last night?" I ask in an effort to get back to the issue at hand.

"Right. My sister." Eileen's shoulders slump and she rests her elbows on the table. "Erin is sixteen and recently got her driver's license. She wanted to visit me so I got it approved for her to stay in the barracks with me. We were having fun and I was showing her around base. We ended up at the commissary to get snacks and as we were leaving, we ran into Jensen and his wife. He—"

"The fucker's married?" Liam shouts and bangs his fists against the table causing Eileen to jump. He pulls himself back off the ledge and takes a few deep breaths to calm down. "Sorry." He glances at me. "You didn't tell me he was married."

"I didn't know," I snap, frustrated at the accusation in his tone. I pin Eileen with my stare. "When did this happen?"

"About a year ago." She tilts her head as if thinking about her answer and then she nods. "Yeah, it was right after the second time he attacked me. I was so happy because I thought that meant it would be over. He had her so what would he want with me, ya know?"

"But it didn't stop."

She shakes her head. "It only made it worse."

"Damn," I seethe. "What happened with Erin?"

"I haven't told anyone in my family about what's going on and I definitely didn't want Erin to pick up on anything. Jensen stopped us and introduced himself to her. She shook his hand. That's the polite thing to do, right?" Eileen's hollow chuckle breaks my heart. "Time stood still. I watched in silent horror as the handshake lasted a beat too long. Apparently, Erin had her own secrets because she started asking him questions about enlisting. I had no idea she was even thinking about that, but it makes sense, I guess. She's always kind of followed in my footsteps, especially since our mom died. Anyway," she waves her hand distractedly. "Jensen told his wife to go on ahead and start grocery shopping without him. She did and that's when he ramped up his game. I listened to Jensen talk about how great it would be to have sisters serving under him, a first in his career. Everything he said had a creepy undertone to it. For thirty minutes, he talked about life on the base, what a typical workday looks like, *inspections,* and Erin ate up every word. Erin knows there are evil people out there but she's naive... one of those people who thinks that nothing bad can happen to them. I was too, if I'm being honest. But bad shit happens to unsuspecting people all the time. Last night, Jensen was a spider weaving a carefully crafted web to catch his prey."

"Did anything happen after that?" I ask.

Again, Eileen shakes her head. "I pretended like nothing was wrong and first thing this morning, I sent her on her way back home. I called in sick and went straight to the closest airport to come here. I knew that I couldn't let any more time pass. If he's going to groom my sister, right in front of me, what is he doing to other people that we can't see? I know there are other women in the military who have suffered at his hand but what about civilians?"

"You did the right thing," Liam assures her in that way of his. That calm, controlled, soothing way.

My thoughts race with this new information. I'd already made up my mind to help and this changes nothing. It just pushes the timetable up. No more being wishy-washy. No more questioning my decision. No more shoving my past deep down and burying it.

No more.

I'm going to end this.

One way or another, Jensen will be stopped and I'll burn his world to the ground.

His reign of terror is over.

20

LIAM

"Thank you for coming."

I glance at Ruby, who's sitting in the chair next to me, Eileen on the other side of her. It's been a week since Eileen showed up at Dusty's, but we've worked quickly since then. We're at an attorney's office in Texas, waiting on the two other women who agreed to come forward. Leslie and Denise are fifteen minutes late and I'm beginning to wonder if Jensen got to them.

"Of course I came" I thread my fingers through Ruby's. "We do this together."

"Right." Ruby glances at her phone, no doubt checking the time again. Her leg bounces so much I can feel it shaking my chair, but I don't say anything. She's nervous and that's okay. I'm here to help with that but I know I can't make it disappear. "Where do you think they are?"

"I don't know."

I pull out my own cell phone and send a quick text to Isaiah.

L & D not here...

Before I can even put my phone back in my pocket, it vibrates with an incoming text.

Isaiah: Has the attorney's office checked on their ETA?

Me: Tried to call… no answer

Isaiah: Give me 10

Me: Thanks

I hold onto my cell, possibilities racing through my mind. No one other than the women, the attorney and club members knew about this meeting. At least not that I know of. Would any of them have taken the chance and told someone? Maybe. But that option doesn't sit right with me. They are all terrified of Jensen and want him to be stopped. I can't believe they'd jeopardize this chance by talking about it outside of a trusted circle of people.

"How much longer do we wait?" Eileen asks.

"As long as it takes," I respond.

Several more minutes tick by and my phone vibrates in my hand.

Isaiah: Get out of there

Immediately, I'm on high alert. I don't waste time by responding. I can do that when we're safe. I stand from my chair as calmly as I can and reach a hand out to Ruby.

"C'mon. We have to go."

Ruby looks at me with confusion creasing the corners of her eyes but doesn't argue. We walk to the front desk and the secretary looks up from her computer.

"Can I help you?"

"We need to reschedule," I say. "The other parties aren't able to make it."

"Okay. I was beginning to wonder. I take it you were able to get a hold of them?"

"Yes," I lie, and I feel Ruby's body tense up. I squeeze her hand to keep her quiet. "They both got called into work and couldn't get away to call. I'm so sorry for the inconvenience."

"Don't you worry about that. I'm just glad everything is okay." The woman is friendly and seems genuinely relieved. I don't know how far attorney-client privilege extends but it seems that even the secretary doesn't have specific details. If she did, she'd be freaking out about the other parties being called into work. "Hmmm, it looks like we have an opening two weeks from today. Does that work?"

I want to scream that no, that's too damn long, but I don't. It's not her fault. "Perfect. Same time?"

"Yes."

"We'll be here. And we'll make sure there are no other delays. Again, we're truly sorry about the inconvenience today." We may have to go back to Indiana first and fly back but that's not her problem.

"Alrighty then. We'll see y'all in two weeks."

I practically drag Ruby from the building, Eileen hot on our heels. I don't slow down until we're in the rental car in the parking garage. Locking the doors, I scan the area around the vehicle, making sure there's no one watching us. I didn't get that sense when we rushed here but one can never be too careful.

"What the hell is going on?" Ruby demands.

"I don't know," I answer honestly. I quickly dial Isaiah's number and push the speakerphone button. "But we're going to find out."

"Are you out of there?" Isaiah asks immediately.

"Yeah. What the fuck, Isaiah? What did you find out?"

"I didn't find out shit. Your dad did. Man's a goddamn genius with computers."

"Yeah, I know." I bite my tongue to keep from lashing out at him. There's no time for extolling the virtues of my father. Not when my blood is boiling and my girl is scared. "What did he find?" I ask with thinly veiled patience.

"Jensen found out about the meeting."

Eileen gasps from the back seat and Ruby punches the dashboard before elbowing the window. Her adrenaline is getting her through this now but she's gonna be hurting later. I make a mental note to get some Advil in her system to at least stave off some of the pain and swelling.

"How is that possible?" Eileen asks when I make no move to continue the conversation. My focus is on Ruby. "All of our communication has been encrypted. I made sure of that."

"You did nothing wrong," Isaiah rushes to assure her. "And everything was encrypted but Jensen got suspicious after you called in sick to come to Indiana. As soon as we realized he'd seen the emails, I texted you back. While we've been waiting to hear from you, Griffin hacked into Jensen's bank records and found money transfers to an offshore account that he traced back to some high-level hacker who gears his particular skills to people in powerful positions. The FBI has never been able to track him down."

"Fine. Great. Jensen's a fucking d-bag and his reach extends to the criminal world too." Ruby's tone is bitter, furious. "What about Leslie and Denise?"

"We're still trying to figure that out," Isaiah admits. "The security camera outside the attorney's office building picked up Leslie's car parking on the street but then it glitches. We couldn't see where she went, if someone else was there, nothing. She just disappeared."

"Ohmigod," Eileen mumbles.

"And Denise?" I'm almost afraid to ask but we need to know.

"Maybe we should talk about this when you get back."

The hesitation in Isaiah's tone gives me pause but it's Ruby who responds.

"No. We're not waiting."

"Are you sure?"

Both Ruby and Eileen nod so I tell Isaiah to go ahead and tell us.

He heaves a sigh. "Griffin ran a search for her name. From what he found, it appears there was an accident late last night."

My blood goes from hot to cold and Ruby's eyes widen. It's Eileen who asks the next logical question.

"What kind of accident?"

"Car accident. Only her vehicle was involved. She went off an embankment on what we assume was her way back to base. From what we can tell, there's no suspected foul play so there won't be an investigation. At least not beyond what is routine to close what they think is an open and shut situation."

"But she's okay?" Eileen asks, hope tinging her words. "You found her in the hospital, right? She's going to be okay?"

Ruby is the one who answers. "No, she's not. She's dea—"

"No!" Eileen shouts. "Don't say that. She's not… no, she's fine." Eileen rips the phone from my palm. "Tell her Isaiah. Tell her she's wrong."

"I'm sorry, Eileen. Denise died on impact." Papers rustle in the background and I hear a loud bang. "Hold on, your dad just walked in and wants to talk to you."

"Son?" My dad's voice comes through the line and Eileen hands the cell back to me.

"Yeah?"

"Are you all somewhere safe?"

"We're in a parking garage down the street from the attorney's office. We were planning on flying back right after the meeting so we didn't make any alternate arrangements."

I should have. I should have had a backup plan. But we didn't think we'd need it. Fly in, meet with the attorney, fly out. What should have been a quick trip is turning into something entirely different.

"Okay. Stay there. I've got our El Paso chapter brought into the loop and they're on their way. They'll escort you to their property. You'll be safe there until we can figure out our next move."

As if on cue, I hear the roar of Harleys and the slight vibration as they rumble through the parking structure.

"They're here."

"Good. I figured it wouldn't be long. A few of the members were already in the city handling a case, but their president assured me that they were done, and he'd send them right away."

"Isaiah, are you okay with this?" I ask, knowing he is but also trying to respect the fact that he's the president and has final say.

"Of course. I asked your dad to reach out while I was talking to you."

"Okay." Six Harley's surround us and a man parks his bike and steps up to my window, signaling for me to roll it down.

"You Liam?" he asks.

"Yeah."

"Danny." He thrusts his hand through the window, and I shake it. "I assume your president let you know we were coming?"

"I did." Isaiah's voice booms through the phone. "I appreciate you acting so fast. Can you get them out of there and to your property? We can continue this phone call once they're safe."

"No problem. Follow us."

Danny straddles his bike and fires it back up. Two bikers pull out and Danny motions for me to follow. I hand the phone to Ruby and start the ignition. When I'm behind them, two others flank our vehicle and Danny and another member take the tail end.

"We'll call you soon," I say to Isaiah.

"Be careful. Keep alert."

"Always."

"Talk soon."

The call ends and Ruby drops the phone into her lap before glancing at me. I don't dare take my eyes off the road as we drive but I can't help but look her way out of the corner of my eye.

"It's going to be okay," I assure her.

She looks back at Eileen, who has been silent in the back seat since the bikers arrived, and then swivels back to face front.

"I'm gonna kill him." Venom practically drips from Ruby's words, a lethal conviction that I haven't heard from her before. "He's not going to get away with this."

"We don't know that this was him," I suggest. I sure as shit don't believe that but I'm trying to keep a cool head until we have all the facts.

"Dammit, Liam!" Ruby slams her fist into the dashboard again. "You know as well as I do that Denise didn't just randomly crash last night. It wasn't a freak accident. It's not a coincidence. Don't placate me by pretending it's anything other than what it is."

"And what is it?" I ask, wanting to see if her thoughts align with mine, although I'm sure I already know the answer.

Before Ruby can respond, Eileen speaks from the backseat, her voice so calm and quiet, it's eerie.

"Murder. Jensen murdered Denise. Shit, he probably has Leslie, too. God only knows if she's still alive."

She leans forward so her head is between the two front seats and looks back and forth between me and Ruby.

"It's time to take a page from his own fucking book."

21

RUBY

"You really should get some sleep."

I roll onto my side and face Liam. We were given a room in the main house of the BRB El Paso chapter and Eileen is just down the hall. Liam has been glued to my side since we arrived and while I appreciate it, I'm about to lose my shit on him because telling me to get some sleep is like telling an alcoholic to quit drinking. It doesn't just happen.

"You're kidding me, right?" I ask with a bite in my tone.

Liam pushes my hair behind my ear and wraps his hand around the back of my head to pull me closer.

"There's nothing more we can do tonight."

I shove away from him and sit up against the wall. "You don't think I know that? That it isn't painfully clear that there's not a damn thing I can do?"

"Ruby, that's not what I said." Liam pushes the blanket off of him and sits up to face me. "There's plenty we can do, plenty we *will* do. *After* we get back to Indiana."

"That's not good enough," I snap. My conscience is shouting at me to stop taking my frustration out on Liam, but I can't stop. Words are flying out of my mouth before I even realize what's happening. "We're just supposed to sleep tonight, tucked in safely, knowing that he's out there, that Leslie is out there? I'm not okay with that and it pisses me off that you are."

"Wait a damn minute," he growls. "I'm not okay with it but I also know that my club is working overtime to track them down so we can get some rest. We're no good to anyone if we're exhausted."

I huff out a breath and cross my arms over my chest. Leaning my head against the drywall behind me, I try to think about where Leslie might be, where Jensen would have her. He's married, so his home is out, unless his wife is equally vile or completely oblivious. I doubt he's stupid enough to keep Leslie on the base, but I know Danny said they were in touch with a contact of theirs to make sure. That leaves... so many fucking places.

"Ya know, Jensen always threatened me and people I cared about. And it scared the hell out of me, obviously." I lift my head and lock eyes with Liam. "But I think a part of me always thought that he'd never take it further than the rapes and destroying careers. How could I have been so stupid? So wrong?"

"Ruby love, you aren't stupid." Liam scrambles to sit next to me and I rest my head on his shoulder. "You're human. I think..."

When he doesn't finish his thought, I bump him with my elbow to encourage him to continue.

He takes a deep breath. "I think you have a good heart and despite what he'd done to you, despite how afraid you were, you wanted to hold onto something good. Believing that he'd only go so far was your way of, I don't know, confining the pain somehow."

"Maybe," I mumble. "I guess it makes sense."

"Look, we can sit here all night and toss out all of the shoulda, coulda, wouldas, but it doesn't change anything. We can't change the past. What we *can* do is let the BRB do their thing and get some rest so we can do whatever we need to do moving forward."

We sit in silence for a few more minutes and eventually, I give in. I scoot to the center of the bed and stretch out. Liam follows suit and pulls the blanket over us.

"I love you, Ruby."

A yawn escapes me and before I can even think about what I'm saying, words fly from between my lips.

"I love you, too."

~

Liam

"I'll send you regular updates on our progress in locating Leslie."

I shake Danny's offered hand and he pulls me in for a back-slapping hug. We only just met but he's family... Brotherhood family.

"I appreciate it. And thanks again for everything." I wrap my arm around Ruby and pull her close to my side. "We'd have been fucked if it weren't for you."

"Nah, you'd have figured it out." Danny chuckles. "You've got skills, Strong. You may not have served as military in war, but you fight a war, nonetheless. Be proud of that."

Danny's words mean a lot, especially from someone who was a Navy Seal, the best of the best.

Ruby pokes me in the ribs with her elbow. "That's what I've told him." She looks up and winks at me. "Maybe now he'll believe me."

Danny throws his head back and laughs. "You snagged a

good one, Strong. Make sure you hold onto her or I just might have to come to Indiana and snatch her up."

"You'll never get the chance."

I shake Danny's hand again and Ruby hugs him as if she's known him her whole life. A sliver of jealousy snakes through me but it quickly disappears when Ruby returns to my side.

"Thanks again," I say over my shoulder as we're walking away.

Eileen is standing at the door, talking with some of the other members and she appears to be blushing. I don't know what that's all about but it's nice to see that she's not completely jaded.

"Ready to go, Eileen?" Ruby asks when we reach the small group.

"As I'll ever be."

We all say our goodbyes and head out to the vehicle. The rental will be returned by the club later today, once we're in the air and far away from this place. Danny is having one of his guys drive us in the shared club vehicle and we'll be flanked by multiple bikes, as well. No chances will be taken.

The ride to the airport is quiet but when we arrive, a flurry of activity quickly ensues. We're greeted by Jasper, an old military buddy of Isaiah's, whose sole job is to get us to the plane without incident. When he leads us to a small terminal, that isn't at all what I'm expecting, my hackles rise.

"This isn't the terminal we're supposed to be in," I observe.

"On paper, no, it's not," Jasper says. "But you've got friends in high places because strings were pulled and the three of you will be traveling on a private aircraft back home."

"Why weren't we notified of this?" I demand, not entirely sure I trust what I'm being told.

"Call whoever it is you need to call to verify what I'm telling you." He thrusts a phone toward me. "But use this. It's secure."

I take the phone and dial Isaiah's number. He answers on the second ring.

"I was wondering how long it would take you to get suspicious."

"So this guy is legit? This change in plans is real?" I ask.

Isaiah chuckles. "You didn't really think I was going to let you stick to plans that would be easy for Jensen to figure out, did you? He's clearly got eyes on Eileen and Ruby and could have easily figured out that plane tickets were purchased for them."

"A heads up would have been nice. All this cloak and dagger shit is getting on my nerves," I snap.

"This 'cloak and dagger shit' is keeping you safe." Isaiah heaves a sigh. "Listen, I didn't tell you because I don't trust that our communication isn't being monitored. Your dad doesn't think it is but why take chances? We've got new phones for all of you when you get back but for now, get on the damn plane."

"We're gonna have a chat when I get home." I look to my left and see Ruby and Eileen watching me, confusion on their faces. "I gotta go."

"Yeah, you do," Isaiah retorts. "See you in a few hours."

I end the call and hand the phone back to Jasper.

"Satisfied?" He quirks a brow at me.

No, I'm not fucking satisfied. I'm pissed off. I'm the VP of the club and my President kept me out of the loop on my own damn assignment. It's not lost on me that he did it to ensure our safety, but it doesn't make it an easier pill to swallow.

"Hardly."

"Well, you better get your head straight because you're

scaring them." He nods to indicate Ruby and Eileen. "Look, we don't know each other, but I know Isaiah. If he kept you in the dark, it was for a damn good reason." He crosses his arm over his chest. "Now, will you please go get on the damn plane?"

I shove a hand through my hair and try to calm myself down. I'm angry, sure, but this guy isn't to blame, and neither are the ladies. I'll deal with the issue at home.

"Thanks for your help." I shake Jasper's hand and turn away from him to head toward Ruby and Eileen. "Ready ladies?"

"Is everything okay?" Ruby asks.

"We're safe, if that's your worry," I reply honestly. "As far as being okay, sure. I'm just going to do a little ass kicking when we get home."

Both Ruby and Eileen laugh off my words and I'm pretty sure it's because they don't believe me. It's hard for people to understand the dynamic of our club, the friendships within it. Most think that because we love one another, we always get along. Just one big happy family.

I rub the side of my nose, my finger brushing the bump that Isaiah caused when he broke it. He took his anger and frustration out on my face and I'm going to do the same.

But in order to do that, we need to board this plane and get the hell out of Texas.

22

LIAM

"Remember, he kept you out of the loop for your own good."

I lower my gaze to take in Ruby and frown. She's supposed to be on my side. But for the last hour, she's been trying to convince me to forget what Isaiah did. Eileen, on the other hand, has remained quiet, speculative. No doubt she's scared, worried about what happens next.

"How are you okay with this?" I demand. "You, of all people, should understand me wanting to know what's going on. With all the crazy rules and stipulations you gave me, you cornered the market on needing control."

As soon as the words leave my mouth, I want to snatch them out of the air and pretend I didn't say them. Ruby rears back and her eyes widen. A split second later, the crack of her palm stings my cheek and seems to echo in the air around us.

"Don't you dare make this about me, Liam Strong!" she shouts and rests her hands on her hips. "You're supposed to be one of the good ones. I gotta say, you're not quite living up—"

"What the fuck is going on?" Isaiah's voice is almost drowned out by the slamming of the door against the house when he shoves it open.

Pent up rage bubbles over and I lunge forward and grab him by his shirt and throw him against the same wall. Pain explodes through my hand when my fist connects with his nose and Isaiah roars as he brings his hands up to ward off any further blows.

"What the fuck were you thinking?" I snarl. "Keeping me in the dark, switching up the plan, acting as if you're the only person with a vote?"

"Liam!" Ruby shouts from behind me. She grabs my arm and I shake her off.

With his hands cupping his nose, Isaiah squares his shoulders and glares at me. "You need to back the fuck off."

"Or what?" I counter, arm pulled back to clock him again.

"Or I'll boot your ass." He drops his hands and blood drips from his fingertips onto the porch of the main house. "You don't like the way I do things, you're free to leave."

I see red. My vision blurs like someone is holding a crimson smoke screen in front of my face. I thrust my fist forward, connecting with his jaw this time.

"Why the fuck would I leave? I'm not a runner. That title is reserved for—"

"Liam Aiden Strong!" I whirl around at the sound of my dad's voice. He's standing there, stone-faced, with my mom at his side. "Don't say something you'll regret."

"Listen to him," Ruby urges. "I know you're angry and on edge. Hell, we all are. But if you could just stop and think for two seconds without your ego getting in the way, you'd recognize that how things were handled was the best way."

I drop my arms to my sides, my chest heaving but my vision clearing. My thoughts remain a garbled mess but the one that pushes its way through is that they're right. If I take my feelings for Ruby out of the equation, I agree with how Isaiah handled the situation.

"Are you done?" Isaiah asks and arches a brow.

I nod, shaking out my fists, the ache settling in my bones now that the adrenaline and anger is wearing off.

"Good." He grins, despite the blood covering his face from his nose down to his chin. "That's the only freebie you're gonna get. Figure I owed you one after I broke your nose." His grin widens and a devilish glint enters his eyes. "I'll leave telling Tillie what happened to my face up to you. Isabelle will probably thank you though. She'll be the better looking twin for a while."

I throw my head back and laugh. Isabelle has always been the better looking twin but I'll let Isaiah have his delusions.

My dad slaps me on the back. "Let's move this party inside." He moves past me and stops when he's shoulder to shoulder with Isaiah. "And Isaiah, ask your father about the time he threatened to kick me out of the club. I think you'll find that, where you two idiots are concerned," he wags his finger between Isaiah and me, "the apples didn't fall far from the trees."

Isaiah's head swivels as he watches my dad walk into the house. When he returns his focus to me, he's frowning. "Any idea what he's talking about?"

I shrug. "I've heard rumors. But they always involve kinky shit about my parents so I've never bothered to ask for the real story."

"Got it. I think I'll pass on asking then."

"I hate to interrupt," Eileen, who's been silently standing at the bottom of the steps since we arrived, steps up next to Ruby. "But it's been a long day and I have to pee. As much as I've enjoyed this little display of machismo, can we, for the love of God, please go inside?"

"I'm sorry, Eileen." Isaiah steps aside to let her pass and

we all follow her in. "Bathroom is right over there, first door on the left down that hall." He points her in the right direction.

"Thanks." She scurries away and the slamming of the door echoes through the large main room.

"I'm going to go clean up my face and I'll meet you in the library. Everyone else is already here."

Isaiah disappears to the room that's reserved for the President in case he ever needs to stay at the main house. I face Ruby and make note of the fact that the fear that's been present for the last week is gone. In its place is anger, likely at me.

"I'm sorry," I say.

She tilts her head. "For what?"

"Being a dick." I reach out to cup her cheek, but she pulls away. "I deserve that I guess. I just… I felt so out of control, like there was nothing *I* could do to protect you. I should've been the one to switch our plans up to keep Jensen off our trail. I should've been the one who found all of that information about him."

"You can't do it all, Liam." She steps closer and wraps her arms around my waist and places her cheek against my chest. "That's why you have your team, your family. So you don't have to."

"I know." I see Eileen re-enter the room out of the corner of my eye and pull back from Ruby and rub my hands up and down her arms. "Let's go get an update."

The three of us make our way toward the library and when we enter, voices die down and all eyes focus in our direction.

"Welcome home," Cooper says with a smile.

"Aw, did ya miss me?" I joke.

"Not you dumbass. But I did miss your girlfriends pretty face."

"Watch yourself," I growl, although there's no real heat behind the words. Cooper is happy with Lila and I know he means nothing by his comment. He just likes to ruffle feathers sometimes.

"Holy shit!" Isabelle exclaims from her spot at the table. "What the hell happened to your face?"

I glance over my shoulder and see Isaiah standing in the doorway, purple and blue marbling his facial features.

"A brick fucking wall happened," Isaiah responds. He makes his way to the head of the table and calls the meeting to a start. He pulls his cell from his pocket and sets it on the table, face up. He presses a few buttons and ringing comes through the line. "First order of business is an update from Danny."

"Yo," Danny answers.

"Danny, it's Isaiah. I've got my members gathered for your update and you're on speaker. Please tell me you have good news."

Danny sighs and I brace myself. "Wish I could, man. Still haven't located Leslie or Jensen. I did have a few of our female members go and shake down the wife. She gave us the location of a rental property that Jensen owns. Says he rents it out fairly cheap. Last tenants vacated a little over a month ago and it's been vacant since."

"Let me guess," I say. "You found the place empty."

"Bingo. But… and this is a big but… there was evidence to suggest that someone was there recently. Coffee pot still had coffee in it, dirty dishes in the sink and trash in the can. Not exactly what you'd expect to find in a vacant rental."

"Any clues as to Jensen's whereabouts or if he was alone when he was there?"

"He wasn't alone. There were two empty toothbrush packages in the bathroom trash."

"Great, the man gives a shit about dental hygiene," Ruby mumbles.

"More disturbing were the used condoms that were with them," Danny informs us.

"He always uses a condom." Eileen sits up straight in her chair, a frown on her lips. "Apparently, he doesn't one hundred percent trust whoever his connections are because he still takes *some* precautions."

"Sick bastard," Isaiah snarls.

"As if I haven't been the bearer of enough bad news, we found something else."

"Jesus, what?" I ask.

"There were several empty syringes. We got lucky and one had a little residue so we were able to test for a substance. Came back as Etorphine."

I've heard of that. Memories claw their way to the surface and when it becomes clear, I whip my head in the direction of my parents. No fucking way.

"Is that…?" I let my question hang in the air, almost too afraid to say it out loud.

"Yeah," Mom says. "That's what was used on me."

My chair crashes to the floor as I shove to my feet, fresh rage swelling inside of me. I scan the faces of everyone in the room and note that not one of them is relaxed. As if the situation isn't bad enough, we now have to contend with the reminder of one of our own's tragic history.

"I sense there's a story there and believe me, I want to hear it, but we need to act." Danny's voice is gritty as it comes through the phone. "If Jensen is drugging Leslie to keep her in line, who knows what else he has in store for her. Liam, can you and your dad do another deep dive into Jensen? Just to make sure we're not missing anything."

"They'll get right on it," Isaiah answers when I remain silent.

"Not to ignore the importance of tracking him down and finding Leslie, but what about the meeting with the attorney?" Eileen looks around the room. "I put this all into motion when I reached out to Ruby and it's not going to end unless we can actually stop him. The attorney can help us do that… legally."

"The meeting stands. In two weeks, you'll all fly back to Texas." Isaiah folds his hands on top of the table and focuses on her. "I was able to get you emergency leave for thirty days. If anyone asks, you had a family emergency that required you to be home to handle it. Hopefully by the time you have to return, Jensen will be in custody."

"Or dead," I sneer.

"We don't break the law," Isaiah reminds me and then shrugs. "Unless we have to."

"Understood." I look at the cell in the middle of the table. "Danny, do you have anything else for us?"

"No. I'll keep giving Isaiah hourly updates. I've got my chapter working around the clock. We'll find them."

"Thanks, Danny," Isaiah says, picking up the phone. "We'll call you with any information we find." Isaiah ends the call and tosses the device down. "Now, what's our plan? Aside from what we're already doing and the meeting, any thoughts on next steps for the two weeks we have before then?"

"I think we should try and track down any other victims," Cooper suggests. "I hate that that means they'll be in danger but at the rate we're going, we're going to need them. We're already down two statements."

"I've got a few women in mind," Ruby says. "I'm not thrilled about the prospect of asking for their help with the obvious danger it puts them in, but I agree with Cooper, we don't have much choice."

"Agreed." My head swivels to my mom at her quick acceptance. "I'll only add that we be very honest and upfront about what coming forward means for them. I also think we need to alert all BRB chapters and bring them in on this case. Jensen has connections and there's no telling how far they reach. We also have no clue where he is. He could be in Texas, on his way here, or in fucking Timbuktu for all we know. The more widespread help we have, the better."

"I'll take care of that as soon as we're done here." Isaiah glances around the table. "Tillie, Lila and Isabelle, you can help."

"What can I do?" Eileen asks.

"We'll put our heads together to find more victims," Ruby says. "Brie, Sadie," she begins, looking at the founding women, "Do you mind helping with that?"

"Not at all," they respond simultaneously.

"Okay," Isaiah booms as he stands. "It's not a complete plan, but it's enough to get us started. Anyone have anything they'd like to add before I close the meeting?"

"I do," I speak up.

"Go for it, VP."

I meet the eyes of every person in the room. "I know this is a bigger villain than we've ever come up against and I know that I'm asking all of you to question a system you've always believed in. It's not lost on me how painful or frustrating that might be. But I appreciate it more than you can imagine. And when this is all over, we're throwing the biggest damn party we can because we'll deserve it."

Cheers erupt from around the table. This is how a system is supposed to work. This is loyalty and friendship and dedication and family.

This is where I shine.

23

RUBY

"I'm sorry but I don't know how I can help you."

I throw the phone across the room when the fifth woman hangs up on me. It shatters when it hits the wall and pieces scatter across the floor. I was so sure there were others but if our success in tracking them down is any indication, I was dead wrong.

"I take it you struck out again?" Brie pushes her laptop to the side and when I nod, she smiles. "Honey, you need to remember how you felt when Eileen first contacted you. You didn't immediately jump on board. You were angry and scared and confused." She looks at Eileen and back at me. "And look at you now. You're both ready to fight. I have a feeling you'd go in guns blazing if you knew where to find Jensen. But that mindset took time. They'll come around."

"She's right," Eileen says from her spot at the desk against the wall. "But even if she's not, we'll be fine. We'll figure it out. We're Army. That's what we do."

"And honestly," Sadie adds, a smirk on her face. "If I have to go ask my son for another burner phone to replace the ones you keep breaking, it won't matter to you if we find Jensen because you'll be dead."

We all laugh at that, as I'm sure Sadie wanted us to. I know she's teasing but she broke the tension in the room and I'm grateful.

"Right." I shrug. "Sorry."

Sadie waves away my apology. "It's fine. Believe me when I say that we understand your frustration. But try to focus that energy on our task. We'll find someone willing to come forward."

With that, Sadie leaves the room and I assume she's going to get that new burner phone she mentioned. We all get back to digging through the military databases that Griffin and Liam were able to hack into to look for all the females who ever served under Jensen. It's a long fucking list and we're going back to the beginning. Leaving no stone unturned.

"Here ya go," Sadie says as she thrusts a flip phone in front of my face. "Liam said to tell you there aren't any left so be more careful." She winks. "We've got an entire box of these things."

"Thanks. I'll try not to need another one."

I return my attention to my laptop to continue scrolling through the documents. Halfway down the screen, a name jumps out at me: Stephanie London. She's the woman who I originally thought was cold, until I realized she was likely dealing with Jensen too.

On the off chance that she has the same number, I dial the digits as I read them out loud. Vibrating excitement rushes through me when it starts ringing.

"Hello?"

"Oh, um, hi." It takes me a moment to sort through my thoughts because I hadn't expected her to answer. "Is this Stephanie London?"

"Who's this?"

"I'm not sure that you'll remember me, but my name is Ruby Banks. We served together at—"

"I know who you are," she snaps, sounding more distracted and shocked than angry. "Look, I'm about to go into a meeting and don't have time for whatever it is you want."

Muffling noises come through the line and I hear her tell someone she'll be right there. When the sound clears, I pounce.

"I know what Jensen did to you." The words fly from my mouth before I can even think them through.

"Hold on."

More muffled noises and then she tells someone to start the meeting without her. Good. I got her attention.

"Give me a second to go outside. I don't need my colleagues hearing all my dark and dirties."

Her footsteps echo through the phone, as if she's jogging down a staircase. I wait for her to get to a place she's more comfortable in and when it takes longer than expected, I start to worry.

"Are you still there?" I ask.

"Yeah. Almost outside." The sound of a door opening and closing reaches me. "Okay, I'm good."

I breathe a sigh of relief and lean back in my chair. I notice that Eileen, Brie and Sadie are all staring at me expectantly and I give them a thumbs up.

"So, Douglas Jensen," she begins. "What do you want to know?"

"Well, for starters, I'm sorry that I never did anything back when everything was going down."

"Ruby, I'm the one who's sorry. I knew what was in store for you and I didn't even try to warn you. I was so wrapped up in my own shit."

"How about we consider today the start of a new era?" I

suggest. "I wanna take him down and I need your help to do it."

"I'm listening."

We spend the next half hour going over everything. I bring her up to speed on Eileen, Leslie and Denise. I tell her about the Broken Rebel Brotherhood and the meeting with the attorney. We end the call with her agreeing to be at that meeting and accepting the protection of the Brotherhood's Seattle chapter until then.

When I set the phone on the table, I feel… light. Which is odd because dealing with a power-abusing rapist is deep, dark shit. But we found someone else to come forward. Jensen's downfall isn't going to rest on my and Eileen's shoulders alone.

"I hate to throw a wrench in your good mood, but I think you should head to the bar tonight. Get some normalcy in your life. Take Eileen." Brie turns to smile at her. "Sadie and I can handle this for now."

"Are you sure?" I ask, frowning. "This isn't your fight. We should be here for every step."

"Ruby, honey," Sadie says. "When are you going to get that you're not alone, you're not responsible for this? You're family and that makes it our fight. We stand with family."

"What she said," Brie agrees. "And I'll go one step further. This fight, this need to stop Jensen? It is our fight because we're women and women don't let other women fight alone."

Tears spring to my eyes at their determination and genuinely good spirit. It reminds me of what I thought I was going to get in the Army but with one big difference: they'll follow through.

~

I arch my back to ease the ache. Between two plane rides in under twenty-four hours, all the stress of the last few days, and being on my feet here at the bar, I'm sore as hell and ready to crawl into bed and sleep for days.

"Last call," I shout to the few remaining patrons.

I wet a rag and start wiping down the bar. Liam clears tables as the last remaining customers leave. I sent Cindy home two hours ago and Eileen is asleep upstairs in my apartment.

Between Liam and I, we manage to shut down in ten minutes. This isn't the first time he's helped me close, and we've perfected our routine. He knows what I'm willing to push off until the next day and what I'm picky about. We make a great team.

At the bar and in general.

Liam sits on a stool and rests his elbows on the bartop. He watches as I gather the cash from the till to put into the safe overnight. His stare is like heat searing my flesh, making me ache and burn in ways that don't involve me sleeping for days.

"Keep that up and I'm going to have to throw Eileen out of my apartment," I say without making eye contact.

"No need to kick her out. I locked the door to the bar."

Liam pushes himself off the stool and leaps over the bar, his eyes never leaving mine. They're dark, deep pools of hunger and he should be required to carry a card he can hand to women to warn them about their lethalness.

When he reaches out a hand to grab my arm, I swat him away. "What are you doing?"

He arches a brow. "I think it's pretty obvious."

"It is but... here? In the bar?"

"I'm thinking more along the lines of *on* the bar, but in the bar works too."

I don't evade him when he reaches for me a second time and I let him lift me and spin around to set me '*on* the bar'.

"You, Ruby love, are so fucking difficult to resist."

He braces his hands at my sides and leans forward, forcing me to either let him capture my lips or lay on my back. I make a quick decision and decide to back away so he has to work a little harder.

He hauls himself up and kneels with his knees on either side of me. I grab his shirt and pull him down, crushing his lips in a bruising kiss. His tongue tantalizes me, taunts me, tempts me. I break contact and lift up to whisper in his ear.

"Fuck me, Liam."

He wastes no time hopping down and dropping his pants. Next, he yanks my pants down to my ankles, where they get caught up by my shoes. I'm dimly aware of the music that still flows from the Jukebox. Before I can even register the song, Liam thrusts into me, scooting me across the wood.

"So fucking good," he growls. "It's always so fucking good."

It's clear that this is going to be quick because Liam applies pressure to my clit, which he knows is the quickest way to get me off. My hips buck and my back arches, my body doing what it involuntarily does to intensify the pleasure.

"Come for me, Ruby." His attention to my clit intensifies. "Come *with* me."

His cock throbs inside of me and I shatter into a million little fragments, each one ricocheting back into place as if drawn to a magnet. Liam collapses on top of me, careful not to crush me.

"I'm going to have to clean the bar again," I say, a teasing lilt to my tone.

"Yeah, sorry about that." He chuckles and then straightens. After he pulls his pants back on, he helps me with mine.

"I'll go grab another thing of disinfectant. I know the bottle under the bar was almost gone."

"Thanks."

When he disappears into the kitchen, where the supply closet is located, I can't stop the smile that curves my lips. I make my way to the Jukebox to turn it off and when I'm back behind the bar, I hear my phone ringing.

I automatically reach for my bag to find my phone and when I realize it's not my personal phone ringing but the burner, I stop in my tracks.

No! Not again. It must be bad if Stephanie is calling at almost two thirty in the morning.

I take a deep breath and answer the call, fully expecting to hear her crying or screaming or something equally terrible. She's the only person who has this number and I told her to only use it for emergencies.

"Hello?"

The silence that greets me is deafening. Liam walks through the doors at that precise moment and rushes to my side when he sees the look on my face. He motions for me to put the phone on speaker, and I do.

"Stephanie? Is that you? Answer me." Panic laces my words.

More silence.

"Stephanie, did he find you? C'mon, give me some kind of sign that you're alive, that you can hear me," I plead.

"Stephanie can't come to the phone right now."

My stomach plummets and my knees go weak because I'd know that voice anywhere. Liam has to hold on to me to keep me from collapsing in a heap on the floor.

"She'll be fine once she agrees to keep her mouth shut like she has all these years." Douglas Jensen chuckles dryly. "But you, dear Ruby… I won't be so forgiving with you."

Liam snatches the phone from my hand and, despite it

being on speaker, holds it up to his mouth. "You stupid motherfucker. You aren't going to do anything to Ruby."

"Oh yeah, big bad biker man?" My eyes widen at that because it means he knows more about Liam than he should. More about me. "You're a goddamned pissant! I'm a well-respected career man with the US Army to back me up. I've been doing what I want, when I want, to who I want for years. You can't possibly think that you and your little gang of military misfits can stop me."

"You're right," Liam seethes, his face red, his shoulders tense. "You have a lot of people by your side, all standing idly by wearing their rose-colored glasses. But what you fail to realize, *pissant*, is I have something you'll never have."

"Oh, please, enlighten me."

"Hundreds of people who have been through hell many times over and have no problem going back if it means stopping you. I have people who actually give a damn."

"We shall see," Jensen taunts. "It's time for me to hang up now." I can hear him snap his fingers. "Oh, and Ruby?"

"What?" I ask, terrified of the answer but needing to know.

"I'm really looking forward to our next... *inspection*."

24

LIAM

"How are we supposed to wait two weeks to meet with the attorney?"

Ruby speaks up to be heard over the voices of the members I roused out of bed with an emergency text. Isaiah, Cooper, Tillie, Lila, Micah, Aiden and my dad all immediately came to the bar so we wouldn't be traveling without backup. I can't help but wonder where Isabelle is, especially with everything going on, but I dismiss that worry as overreaction. Noah and Jace are still in position outside, keeping an eye on things.

"We don't," I growl. "We act now."

"Liam, son, you're not thinking clearly." My dad tries to place his hand on my shoulder and when I pull away from him, he sighs and turns to face Isaiah. "My two cents, for what they're worth, is to stay the course. We've already filled in all chapters about Stephanie. Let them do their thing to help so we can keep our focus on finding as much info as we can and other victims."

"No more victims," Eileen says before Isaiah has a chance to respond. "I refuse to put anyone else in even more danger than they already are." She scrubs her hands over her face, and I note that they're shaking. "Maybe we should just let it go. Jensen wasn't kidnapping and killing people before. As long as we keep our mouths shut, we'll be fine."

"Fuck that!" Ruby shouts. "Eileen, if you want to back out, I get it. And you'll get no judgement or backlash from me or anyone else in this room. But I'm all in. I'm seeing this through till the end, no matter the consequences."

"Why is it our job to make him stop?" Eileen cries. "Why are we responsible for shining a light on what he's done? It's not fair."

"You're absolutely right, it isn't fair. But it's our responsibility because we're the only ones willing to do it." Ruby shrugs. "We're the only ones."

"Eileen, you don't need to decide tonight," I assure her, although resentment bubbles just beneath the surface because she's the one who set this all in motion. She's the one that came looking for a fight. I'll follow Ruby's lead and let Eileen do what she wants but there's a big part of me that wants to demand she stick with it.

"Maybe we don't need the attorney," Isaiah says.

"How do you figure?" I demand. "We need someone who can back the victims in a legal battle."

Isaiah turns to Tillie. "We have an attorney."

"You want to compromise your own wife's safety?" Aiden barks. "My daughter's safety?"

"I'll do it," Tillie says quickly, before protests of the idea can get out of control.

"No, absolutely not!" Aiden shouts.

"Dad, it's not your decision."

"Bullshit," he snaps at her and glares at Isaiah. "I won't allow her to be put in the middle of this mess. I swear to Christ if you don't toss this idea right out the window, I'll—"

"You'll what?" Isaiah asks. "Do you really think this is a

decision I'd make lightly? I don't want Tillie in danger either, but I hate to break it to you, she's already knee deep, just by being connected to us."

Isaiah and Aiden are standing toe to toe so I step in between them and push them apart. We have enough to contend with and the last thing we need is dissension among our own. Aiden struggles against me but Isaiah simply backs away and takes his place next to Tillie, throwing an arm around her and pulling her close.

"I'm doing this," Tillie confirms. "With Jensen's rapid escalation, I doubt it'll come to the point where I'm needed in any legal capacity. But at least with me as the attorney, we can keep this whole case in-house. We can hold meetings here or at another chapter location. We control what happens. Not him."

"She's right," I agree on a sigh. When Aiden glares at me, I hold a hand up to keep him silent. "I don't like it either. Hell, I don't like any bit of this whole thing, but we're running out of options unless we put execution on the to-do list."

"I'm good with that," Ruby snaps.

"Me too," Eileen agrees.

"Yeah, well, call me crazy, but I'm not," I retort. "I want the bastard dead, don't get me wrong, but I don't want taking a life on my list of things that keep me up at night." I reach out and tilt Ruby's head up to look at me. "And I don't want that for you either."

Ruby's eyes fall closed, exhaustion evident in the dark circles marring her cheeks. She's still the most beautiful woman I've ever seen but I vow to make that darkness, both physical and mental, go away.

"I'm glad we seem to be coming to some sort of agreement but I'm going to throw a wrench in things."

All eyes turn to Cooper, who has been silent since arriving. As the newest member of the family, and the most recent of us to watch the love of his life suffer, I'm curious about his thoughts.

"Spit it out," Isaiah says.

"Jensen has escalated, right?" We all nod. "He's also taken his criminal activities over state lines. Murder and kidnapping in Texas, kidnapping in Seattle, threats in Indiana. This is a federal case now. But even more than that, at the core of it all, it's a military issue."

"The military didn't do—"

"I know," Cooper agrees before Ruby can finish her sentence. "But surely between all of the club chapters, we have just as many high-ranking connections in the Camouflage Caravan. Let's use them."

I fight a grin at Cooper's nickname for the military and glance down at Ruby. "I know we wanted to work our way up to that, but Cooper's right. We need to quit trying to do it all ourselves and beat Jensen at his own game. He thinks he's untouchable because of his rank and standing in the Army but he's not."

"Are you ladies okay with that?" Isaiah asks. "If you are, I'll do an emergency conference call with every chapter president and get the ball rolling."

Ruby and Eileen glance at each other, silently coming to a decision. When they return their attention to Isaiah, they nod and speak in unison. "Do it."

"Consider it done." Isaiah glances around the room. "I know you're all tired, but I don't see a lot of sleep in our future. Take the rest of the night and get as much shuteye as you can. We'll reconvene at ten, in the library back home."

I watch as each person files out of the front door of the bar and when it closes after the last one, I notice that Isaiah didn't leave with them.

"Is there something else?" I ask as I rub the back of my neck to ease some of the tension.

Isaiah reaches into his pocket and pulls out a flip phone, one of the burners. He thrusts it at Ruby. "Here. Your other phone is compromised now. Take out the battery and toss it."

She grabs the phone, holding it in her hand like a lifeline. "Thanks."

"Don't mention it. At least you didn't break another one." Isaiah makes his way to the door. "I'll see you guys in a few hours. Get some sleep."

When he disappears through the exit, Ruby slumps against the booth next to her and exhales loudly, the phone still gripped in her hand. I glance at Eileen, who's sitting at a table a few feet away and her chin is resting in her palm. Both of these women need closure, some form of justice that lets them walk away as unscathed as possible.

But even more than that, they need sleep. And that is something I can give them immediately. I lock up the bar, waving to Noah and Jace who are still parked in the lot, keeping watch. I toss the few empty glasses strewn around from the club into the dirty dish pan and make a mental note to get up early and wash them before Ruby has to deal with it.

"C'mon ladies," I urge. "Let's get upstairs and get some shut-eye."

They both silently stand and make their way to the back staircase. I follow them up, making sure to lock the apartment when we're inside. Eileen flops down on the couch and Ruby goes straight to the bed.

"Do either of you need anything?"

"I'm good," Eileen responds around a yawn.

"Just you," Ruby says.

I look out the window and assure myself that all is quiet in the world around us. Secure in the knowledge that, at least for the next few hours, we're safe, I crawl into bed beside Ruby and wrap my arm around her.

She scoots backward, curling up against me as the little spoon does. Within minutes, her breathing evens out and her muscles relax, telling me she's asleep. Unfortunately, I can't shut my brain down as fast.

I stare at the wall, the phone call from Jensen playing in my mind, over and over and over. How Ruby survived him, I have no clue.

Yeah, you do. She's so fucking strong.

And even though I hold on to that thought, it's another two hours before it lulls me into a restless sleep.

25

RUBY

I rub my temples to ease the dull, throbbing ache that's plaguing me. Eileen and I have been rehashing all the horrid details of our time with Jensen for the last five hours. Tillie has patiently listened, taking copious notes despite the recorder that's on the coffee table in front of us.

"We can take a break," Tillie says.

"No, we're almost done." I sit up straight. "I wanna finish up before Liam and the guys get back."

Liam, Isaiah, and Cooper are at the club, trying to coordinate everything with each BRB chapter. After speaking with all chapter presidents, Isaiah scheduled a larger video conference with all patched members, so any and all questions or concerns could be addressed. They expected it to last a while, but it's already been two hours since it started and I'm not entirely sure what constitutes a 'while' to them.

"Okay." Tillie leans forward on the couch, her head down as she reviews what she's written in her notebook. "Do you remember the name of the person you reported the first incident to, Ruby?"

I shake my head. "No. I went to the MPs on base but when they turned around and told Jensen who made the report, I think I just blocked the whole thing from my mind."

"No worries. I'll have Liam or Griffin dig through their records and see if they can find the original report. It's not imperative to know who you spoke with, but it would help to be able to show exactly where in the system you were failed."

"Something to keep in mind is, whoever took the report, they're clearly not one of the good guys. If they gave a damn about me or what was going on, they wouldn't have gone to Jensen the way they did."

"I understand that, but we still need to be able to give as much detail as possible." She turns to Eileen, who's sitting cross-legged on the floor, leaning against the coffee table. "Did you ever report the rapes to anyone?"

A look of shame washes over Eileen's face. "I tried. It didn't go as planned and I never tried again. Besides, Jensen was my boss. And I wanted nothing more than to be in the Army. I didn't want to do anything to jeopardize that."

"Okay. No worries. This is just further evidence of how he manipulates his victims." Tillie flips through the pages, her lips moving as she silently reads. When she slams the notebook closed, she tosses it next to the recorder and then presses the stop button. "I think I've got everything I need for now. Isaiah has already spoken to an MP officer he knows and he's standing by to help. He's also bringing in two JAG officers that he trusts."

"Does Liam trust them?" I ask, that being more important to me than if some unknown MP trusts them.

"Isaiah trusts the MP and the MP trusts the JAG officers." She shrugs. "And Liam trusts Isaiah so I'm gonna say, yes, Liam trusts them."

It all seems so convoluted, and I've been burned one too

many times, but I trust Liam and I know that he wouldn't put me in any further unnecessary danger so I accept her rationale.

A knock on my door startles us all and I jump up to answer it. When I throw the door open, Isaiah is standing there with an angry look on his face.

"Don't ever do that again," he growls.

"What?"

"Answer the door without knowing who's on the other side."

"I knew it was you," I say, knowing full well I didn't.

Liam brushes past me and gripping my arm, pulls me away from the door. He slams it shut and flips the lock with choppy movements and I realize just how angry he is. When he yanks me toward him and holds me tightly against his chest, it dawns on me that it's not anger he's displaying, it's fear

"I'm sorry," I say, my voice muffled by his shirt.

"Me too," he says into my hair. "It's just... dammit Ruby, I can't lose you. I need you to be more careful."

I simply nod, knowing that words aren't necessary.

He urges me away from him and guides me toward the couch, where Tillie and Eileen are watching the scene unfold.

Liam's face sobers. "I've got some news." He takes a deep breath. "Danny and his team found Leslie."

My hand flies to my mouth and Eileen gasps. I shake my head, back and forth, back and forth, silently begging for him to tell us something other than what I know is coming.

"It looks like she died of an overdose from that shit he was pumping into her." Liam steadies me when my body sways. "Her death has been reported to local police and an investigation is being opened. There was no way for them to get around reporting it. Not that we want them to," he rushes to add. "But they have listed Jensen as a suspect, based on the information Danny provided them, and they've issued a BOLO. There's no way Jensen won't hear about it, not with his connections."

"Now what?"

"I'm tempted to say let the police handle it and take him down for us. Isaiah and I spoke to the detective in charge and handed over what we knew about him crossing state lines and Stephanie. The FBI will be looped in. It won't be long before he has nowhere to hide. The hunter will become the hunted."

"Does this mean it's over?" Eileen asks.

"No." Liam shakes his head. "It just means that we stick to our plan but hand over any info we obtain to the cops. Maybe, with them on board, it can end faster. There's no way that he's charged as a civilian. Once he's found, his life is over. I'm not confident that he'll stay tucked away, wherever he is, but I don't think it'll be long until we all can rest a little easier."

"This is good news," Tillie says, hope in her tone.

"Is it?" I snap. "Jensen has been getting away with whatever he wants for how long? Ten years? Twenty? What makes you so sure that the law will get their thumbs out of their asses and stop him?" I stomp to the kitchen and pull the tequila bottle out of the cabinet, along with a tumbler. I pour myself a healthy amount and toss it back like it's water. "I can't be the only person who ever reported him. And I sure as hell don't believe his perverse behavior started when he joined the military, which means he likely raped women when he was younger. I'm going to assume at least one of them told *somebody*. And yet, here we are!"

I pour another glass and down it quickly. Liam steps up beside me and takes the bottle from my grasp and puts it back in the cupboard. He then grabs the glass and rinses it out in the sink.

"I know you're angry, but tequila isn't going to help. Certainly not at," he pulls his cell from his pocket and looks at the time, "two in the afternoon."

"I'm not angry," I counter, loudly. "I'm fucking livid! How does this happen? How are people okay with letting women be silenced?" My shoulders slump. "How am I supposed to be okay without getting revenge for what he did to me?"

"Aw, Ruby love," Liam says softly, pulling me into his arms. "You're not. And there are plenty of good people who aren't okay with it. Those are the people that we're counting on. Those are the people you have in your corner."

I swallow past the lump in my throat and choke back the tears. Jensen hasn't touched me in years, yet he's still winning. He's still breaking me without hardly trying.

"I don't know how much longer I can do this, Liam. I want a normal life. I want..."

Liam says nothing, simply stands there and holds me. I hear footsteps and feel a hand on both of my arms. I lift my head enough to see that Eileen and Tillie have flanked me, surrounded me with support.

"What do you want, Ruby?" Tillie asks.

I think about my answer. It's not that I don't know what it is, but how do I put into words what I'm terrified will never happen?

"I want..." I take a deep breath and step back so I can look at all of them. "I want to be with Liam without all the other shit mucking it up. I want Jensen to be stopped. I want to see my family again, go home and give them a hug. I want to not have to look over my shoulder, wondering if today is going to be the day he gets me. I want other women to join the military because it's their dream and not have it turn into their nightmare. I want to stop feeling crazy or like my life is constantly spinning out of control. I want love and happiness and friends."

As I speak, tears spill over my lashes and flow down my cheeks. I wipe them away with shaky hands and force myself to stand tall.

"I fucking want *normal*."

26

JENSEN

On a beach in Florida…

"Do you have any idea the shit I'm dealing with here?"

I roll my eyes at Larry's outburst. He's been complaining for twenty minutes about everything under the sun and I'm getting bored. I glance toward the beach house I rented, under a fake name of course, and feel my lips tug up when I see Stephanie on the lounger by the private pool. I spent good money to get a house that didn't come with neighbors but even if it had, she's so drugged that anyone who sees her will just think she's enjoying a day in the sun.

"Doug, are you even listening to me?"

My temper sparks when he uses my first name. He knows I hate being addressed as anything other than Jensen. My daddy always told me that if people only address you by your last name, it's a sign of respect… or fear. Both are fine with me.

"I'm listening. I'm bored and you're being dramatic, but I'm listening."

I dig my feet into the sand and lean back in my beach chair like I haven't a care in the world, as he keeps droning on. "There's a BOLO out for you." He lowers his voice to a whisper. "For murder."

"I'm aware."

"Look, I've covered for you for years. I'm made every report dis—"

"I've paid you well for all of it so don't pretend that you're not getting something out of our arrangement. I'm pretty sure that Sally would have left your sorry ass long ago if she no longer lived in the lap of luxury."

"She's not with me for my money," Larry huffs.

"Keep telling yourself that." I take a sip of the Mai Tai I've been nursing, the cold liquid sliding down my throat and cooling me. "Can we get back to the issue at hand? Without all the yelling and hysterics?"

"I don't know what you expect me to do. If you think I've been able to handle keeping you out of trouble all these years on my own, you're delusional. And every single member of my team is out."

I sit up so fast that my drink sloshes over my hand. I toss the remaining contents into the sand and throw the glass. "What do you mean, they're out? And who are 'they' exactly?"

Despite what he thinks, I'm not delusional. I've known for years that he put together a team to help. I made sure that he was compensated enough so he could pay them, and I never asked who they were because the weaker the direct connection I had to them, the better. it's worked out well for me... until now.

"I mean, that no amount of money in the world is going to keep them on. They've all risked a lot for you, but they're done. When it was just diddling a few women here and there, that was one thing. None of us liked it but at the end of the day, they all still got to go on breathing. But murder? Jesus

Christ, Doug, there are just some lines that people won't cross. Congratulations, you found theirs. And mine."

I see my carefully crafted existence flash before my eyes. Larry thinks that he can just walk away from this, that he says he's out and I'll let him go? He doesn't know me as well as he should.

"Say, Larry, how *is* Sally these days? Is she still going to spin class three times a week? Still doing her daily yoga routine?" I pause for effect and when I hear a loud thud, like someone hitting something hard, I know I've got him. But I might as well twist the knife, just a little bit more. "She's always been a beautiful… *tempting* woman. Maybe it's time I visit and see for myself."

"Leave my goddamn wife out of this!" He yells. "Even you wouldn't bite the hand that feeds you."

"That's just it, Larry, I'm not." Every single ounce of tension drains from my body and I'm as giddy as a kid on Christmas morning. "I mean, you did say you're done feeding me."

A string of very colorful language spews through the speaker and a laugh bubbles up my throat.

Checkmate motherfucker.

"What do you need me to do?" Larry grudgingly asks.

"I'm afraid it's not that easy, Larry. You've pissed me off, threatened to stop helping me. I'm glad to see you've come around to see things a little more clearly, but it's going to cost you."

"How much?"

In my mind's eye, I can see him sitting at his desk, fat and seething with his jaw set and his thinning hair standing on end from him pulling on it through his anger. Yeah, I'm positively jubilant.

"I think you mean, how little."

"What's that supposed to mean?"

"It means, asshole, that you're gonna figure out a way to clear my fucking name and you're gonna do it for free and with a fucking smile on your chubby face."

I stand up and turn in a circle, seemingly able to see for miles. I like it here. It's peaceful, calm, remote. It'd be a perfect place to retire or start over. And Jane would love it too. Not that I give a damn about her preferences. At the thought of my wife, I make a mental note to call her when I'm done with Larry.

"I can't do it fo—"

"You can and you will," I snap. "Sally deserves that, don't you think?"

I pull the phone away from my ear, chuckling at his shouting, and disconnect the call. I snap the cheap flip phone in half and walk to the water and throw it in. Good luck using that to track me.

On my way back to the ramp that leads to the house, I pick up my towel and the fanny pack I brought with me. The thing is tragic, but it helps me blend in. I unzip the front pocket and pull out a second phone, one I always carry and that is registered under a different name. The only person with the number is my wife.

As I'm walking, I tap her name on the screen and lift the phone to my ear.

"Douglas, my love, I was just about to call you."

Jane's voice goes through me like fork tines scraping a metal plate. I cringe but force an appropriate amount of cheer into my tone.

"Beat ya to it," I say, rolling my eyes. "I miss you."

"I miss you too my love."

"How are your parents doing?"

When I found out that those stupid bitches, Ruby and Eileen, were plotting against me, I sent Jane for an extended stay with her parents, who've retired in Italy. She didn't put up much of a fight but did go on and on about how she hated that I couldn't go with her. Fortunately, she didn't link the women who came to our house and questioned her to my reason for sending her away. Jane's gullible and bought my story about some property ownership survey being conducted among high-ranking military officials.

"They're doing wonderful. They wish you were here." She lowers her voice. "I do too."

"I know, honey, but you know how the Army is. They needed someone with my experience to head this mission and there was just no way out of it."

"I know, I know. I can't wait until you retire next year and we can travel and do things together like a normal couple."

She knows nothing about what I really do in the Army. Basically, I ride a desk and bark orders. Oh, and inspections. That's the best part. And I have no plans to retire or at least I didn't. This little witch hunt may change my plans but that's yet to be determined. My fate depends on how well Larry cooperates.

"The year will pass quicker than you think," I say.

I step off of the ramp onto the concrete that bridges the rest of the way to the rental house's back gate. Stephanie is only a few feet away and the closer I get, the more aware of her I am. As Jane rambles on about all of the 'adventures' she wants to take me on, my cock hardens because I'm thinking about the woman lounging by the pool.

I lift the hatch and see Stephanie struggling to sit up. I reach into the fanny pack and grab the prefilled syringe, flicking it to rid it of air bubbles.

"Honey, I've gotta go," I say into the phone. "Duty calls."

I disconnect the call, knowing that I'm going to pay dearly for it the next time we speak but not caring enough to second-guess the action.

"Hey, sleeping beauty." I close the distance between

Stephanie and me, slowly, carefully so as not to startle her. "I was wondering when you were going to wake up and enjoy your vacation."

She lifts her head and her eyes widen a fraction of a second before I jab the needle into her neck and depress the plunger, pumping her full of more drugs to knock her out. As the toxin takes effect, I put my arm around her and gently ease her back onto the lounger.

"There ya go," I say.

I shove my hand into my shorts as I stand and grip my cock, squeezing and pumping to keep it hard. I throw my head back and close my eyes, envisioning her mouth wrapped around my length.

"Now we can both enjoy our vacation."

27

RUBY

One week later...

"I'm going to head on home if you're cool to close up."

I smile at Cindy and wave her away. She's worked her ass off covering for me as we do all we can to track Jensen down. I came into Dusty's tonight because I needed a break, something to distract me.

"Thanks again for pulling all these extra shifts," I say to her when she reaches under the bar to grab her bag. "I appreciate it."

"Don't mention it. The additional tips alone make it worth it." She winks at me and laughs. "Seriously, though, I'm happy to do it. I don't know exactly what's going on but if extra shifts are how I can help, count me in."

I wring out the rag in my hand and shake off the excess water before starting to wipe down the bar.

"You're a good friend," I say, not meeting her eyes. I know I've said things that can't be taken back but she's been great, pretending like the night I pushed her away never happened.

"I know." She throws her arms around me in a hug I'm not expecting. "See ya tomorrow."

And with that, she's gone. Liam takes her place behind the bar and he's shaking his head.

"What?" I ask.

"You should have seen the look on your face when she hugged you. It was a hug, Ruby, not a shot at the doctor's office."

"I'll have you know, I don't mind shots," I snap back, no heat in my tone. "I'm just not used to hugs. Not that I didn't grow up getting them or that I don't like them but, in case you haven't noticed, I haven't exactly had the best track record with people."

"Even me?" There's a teasing quality to his question but I can't help but wonder if he really needs reassurance.

"You, Liam Strong, are the one person I've gotten it right with. May have taken me a while, but you waited me out." I shrug one shoulder like it's no big deal. "I love you. I don't think I knew what love was until I met you. Not romantic love anyway."

He steps in close and leans in until he's inches from my face. "I love you too."

He presses his lips to mine, slanting his head for better access. I grip the waist of his jeans and hold on to him for dear life. He kisses me so deeply, so hungrily, that I forget where we are. And then a cell phone rings, snapping me out of my trance.

I break contact and take a step back, pulling my bottom lip in between my teeth. The phone keeps ringing, and it dawns on me that it's the ringtone on my own cell. My burner cell.

"That's my burner."

Liam's eyes narrow. "Who has that number?"

"No one that I know of."

"Well, are you going to answer—"

The ringing stops.

"Never mind." Liam reaches around me and grabs the phone from my back pocket. He flips it open and stares at the screen. "I don't recognize the number." He turns it to face me. "You?"

I read the number several times, trying to get something to click, but it doesn't.

"It's an El Paso area code," I observe and lift my head to look at him. "A detective maybe?"

"I guess it could be, but I still don't know ho—"

The phone begins ringing again and I jump at the sound. Liam, on the other hand, stiffens with tension. Rather than having me answer it, he does it himself.

"Hello?" I can't hear the other half of the conversation. "Yeah, she's right here." He hands me the phone and mouths the word 'detective'.

I tentatively grab the phone and place it against my ear.

"Hello."

"Is this Ruby Banks?" the voice on the other end asks.

"Y-yes. How did you get this number, detective?"

"Oh, ma'am, I'm sorry. I'm not a detective. I just told him that so he'd give you the phone."

My spine stiffens and I lock eyes with Liam. I motion him to follow me and head through the doors to the kitchen so I can put the phone on speaker.

"Who the fuck is this?" I demand when I'm certain my customers can't overhear.

"You're a hard woman to track down."

"She asked you a goddamn question," Liam barks.

There's a beat of silence and then a long indrawn breath.

"I'm the man who's going to help you take down Douglas Jensen."

~

"It could be a setup."

I look toward Cooper and shake my head. "I don't think so. He knew so much. Hell, he knew *everything*. Dates, names, places. He was able to list every single time Jensen attacked me." I take a deep breath and turn my head to speak to Isaiah. "Liam and I did some digging before we called this meeting. Larry Carpenter is who he says he is. Decorated five-star General of the United States Army. He's been cleaning up Jensen's messes for years."

"Why?" Isaiah asks.

"That was pretty much my response." Liam grabs his laptop and, after a few keystrokes, he turns it for Isaiah to see. "Then we found this."

Isaiah's lips move as he skims over the screen. "Well, fuck."

"Exactly," I exclaim. "Jensen saved Carpenter's life when they were both newbies, over in Afghanistan. Jensen's been calling in favors ever since." I grin. "It doesn't hurt that Carpenter's made millions off of Jensen for his trouble."

"Money talks." Liam smiles like a cat that caught a canary. "We've got him."

Isaiah holds up his hands. "Look, I hope that's what this means. But you both know as well as I do that Cooper has a point. This could all be a setup. Just because everything looks good and legit doesn't mean it is. Isn't Jensen proof of that?"

I don't let their doubt burst my bubble, but I do temper my excitement. As much as I hate to admit they're right, they're right. But I have a good feeling about this.

"How do we determine if it's a setup?" I ask, needing to know now so this can be over.

"Is he willing to meet with you?" Cooper asks.

"He is," Liam responds. "He told us to name the time and

place and he'd make sure he's there."

"That's promising," Isaiah confirms. "He's not demanding he set the location, which is usually a good sign."

"That's what I said," I breathe.

"Why is he coming forward now?" Cooper asks.

"That he wasn't as forthcoming about," I admit, my shoulders slumping.

"Then let's see if we can convince him to share." Isaiah points to the phone in my hand. "Call him."

I flip open the device and click on the number from the last call and then the speaker button. I hold it, face up, so we can all hear.

"Yes?" Larry says in greeting.

"This is Ruby. I've got Liam, the guy from earlier, and a few others in the room that have questions. Is this a good time?"

"Any time devoted to knocking Jensen down a peg is a good time. What can I do for you, Miss Banks?"

"Sir, my name is Isaiah Mallory. If you want to check me out, feel free. You'll find a clean military record and honorable discharge." Isaiah speaks with authority, but also a hint of the respect that is drilled into military members for five-star generals.

"That won't be necessary. I already know all I need to know about you and the Brotherhood."

Isaiah and Liam's eyes widen. This is new information to all of us, but if I'm being honest, I'm not surprised. If he's to be believed, Larry has been Jensen's cleaner for years and would make it his business to know everything he possibly can.

Getting to the reason for the call, Isaiah asks, "Why are you coming forward now?"

Larry heaves a sigh. "That's a good question, son."

"No offense, sir, but I'm not your son. I have a father. One who would never dream of covering for a man like Jensen." Isaiah pauses. "Sir."

"No offense taken. You're right," Larry admits. "I've covered up some horrible things. And I have to live with that forever. I'm not proud of it and I won't make any excuses for it."

"Then I'll ask again," Isaiah counters. "Why the sudden change?"

Larry heaves a sigh. "Let's just say that Jensen has turned what was a lucrative business arrangement into something personal."

I bite my tongue, trying to keep myself silent as he talks about what happened to me, and so many others, as a 'lucrative business arrangement'. The copper taste of blood fills my mouth, but I ignore it.

"What's in it for you?" Cooper asks. "Oh, sorry, sir. This is Cooper Long. You won't find any military records on me but if you and Jensen are the likes of who I'd have had to serve under, I'm good with that."

Larry ignores the jab and addresses the question. "I'm not a stupid man. I know that Jensen can bury me if he wants to. But I'm less than six months from retirement, I have a wife that I love, and a reputation that I'm proud of. I'll help you and we can bring all of this to an end quickly, but I need you to assure me of one thing first."

"What's that?"

"Ideally, I'd like to keep my actual part in everything hidden but I know that's not a promise you can make." He pauses and breathes deeply. "I'll settle for making sure my wife is taken care of if I go to prison. I don't want her to have to deal with any blowback. Assure me of that and you've got me."

"Done."

All eyes turn to Liam, questioning his response. He only

shrugs. Larry's sigh of relief is loud and long.

"Good. Now," he pauses and shuffling papers can be heard. "Name a time and location and I will bring everything I have on Jensen."

"We'll send you a time and coordinates when we're ready."

Isaiah ends the call and sets the phone on the table.

"Are you satisfied?" I ask, glancing between Isaiah and Cooper.

"For now," Cooper responds. "How quickly can we make this meeting happen, Pres?"

"Tomorrow morning. I'm not willing to wait any longer in case this is a set up. The less time he has to plan something with Jensen the better." He turns to Liam and me. "I'll send you the exact time and coordinates and when you receive them, forward them to the General immediately."

"Got it."

"Keep your phone on you at all times. It may be the middle of the night when you get something from me."

"Done."

"VP," Isaiah rests a hand on Liam's shoulder. "Stay alert. Stay with Ruby. Eileen has been spending time with some of the guys. They make her feel safe. I'll give her the option of staying with them or coming to stay with the two of you."

"Sounds good. You know I won't let Ruby out of my sight."

"I know." He drops his arm. "Hopefully this will all be over soon."

My gut is screaming at me that this is it. I'm sure of it. Jensen is done. Whether or not we can save Stephanie remains to be seen but at least Jensen will be stopped and unable to hurt anyone else.

"It will be," I say, my voice strong and confident. "It has to be."

28

LIAM

"I can't believe this could be over today."

I lift Ruby's hand and kiss her palm. We landed in Texas an hour ago and are sitting in the El Paso chapter's great room in their main house, waiting on Larry to arrive. We debated about whether or not to give him a club address but decided we were better guarded on our own territory.

"You know that getting the information from Larry doesn't end things, right?" I hate to stifle her optimism, but I want her to be realistic. "Jensen is still out there and until he's caught, we still need to be careful."

"Buzzkill," she accuses, causing a chuckle from me.

"I'm sorry, Ruby love. I'm trying to stay positive and you're right, today will bring us a giant step closer to it all being over. Just not all the way." I squeeze her hand to punctuate my statement, letting her know that I'm still here, as always, but I'm being cautious.

The door opens and Danny walks in, with Isaiah at his side.

"He's here," Danny informs us. "Are you ready?"

"Bring him in," I reply.

It was decided that the only people in the room for this meeting would be Ruby, Isaiah, and myself. The less people in the room to spook him, the better. We need what he says he can give us.

While Danny goes to bring Larry to us, Isaiah sits in the chair to my left. Ruby is on my right. Ruby's knee bounces under the table with nervous energy but stops when I rest my hand on her thigh. I can practically feel the tension coursing through her veins but, when she puts her mind to it, she's incredible at hiding it on the surface.

Two minutes later, Danny ushers Larry into the room. Isaiah and Ruby stand and salute, no doubt the act so ingrained in them, they didn't even think about it. I, on the other hand, have no such training and remain seated. This is not a man I want to give my respect to. I don't give a shit what good he may have done for our country. He covered for Jensen, which makes him just as dirty.

"At ease," Larry instructs and Ruby and Liam sit back down.

While Larry gets situated, I take the time to size him up. He's not a small man by anyone's standards but it's clear that he's not as fit as he probably once was. Based on our research, he's in his sixties, a fraction of the fight left in him that he once had. His face is round, his hair thinning. Sure, we saw a picture of him when we first checked into his story, but it must have been an older one because he's a pudgier, older, sadder version of what I was expecting.

"Please, sir, have a seat." Isaiah indicates the one lone chair across the table from us. We purposely removed all of the other chairs, other than the four we are using, in an effort to keep him where we want him. "Before we get started, I need to let you know that we're going to be recording this meeting, at the advice of our attorney. If that's going to be a problem, then you're free to leave."

Larry bristles under his uniform but quickly masks his annoyance. "As long as you hold up to your end of the deal, that's fine."

"I assure you, we aren't the ones at this table who wouldn't keep their word," I retort.

Larry says nothing to that and instead, pulls a file out of his briefcase that is no less than two inches thick. Then another and another. When he's done, he pushes them across the table and pulls out another three that look identical in size.

"That is an entire paper trail documenting every incident and what was done to cover it up. You'll find details regarding payments received by me, from Jensen, along with any payments I made to others when I required assistance." He takes a deep breath. "You'll also find copies of every false identity he's used when he needs to keep hidden, bank account numbers, addresses, all communication between us… everything."

"Names of victims?" Ruby asks, flipping through the pages.

Larry nods. "All thirty-six of them."

Ruby's head whips up. "Th-thirty-six?"

Larry's face falls and for the first time since he walked in the room, he looks genuinely ashamed of his part in all of this. "Yes. I can name every single one by memory if you'd like."

"That won't be necessary," I inform him.

I glance at Ruby and note that her cheeks are pale and the shock at learning the number of victims isn't going to wear off any time soon. She always suspected there were a lot more women, but I don't think her mind let her go to that high of a number.

"Of course, my knowledge and information doesn't extend beyond his time in the Army."

"You didn't dig into his past?" Isaiah asks.

Larry shakes his head. "I probably should have, but I didn't want to know."

"What number am I?" Ruby asks quietly, staring at the files and seemingly not aware of the continued conversation around her.

"Excuse me?"

She lifts her head and locks eyes with Larry. "What. Number. Am. I?"

There's a beat of silence before Larry responds. "Twenty-nine."

"Twenty fucking nine!" Ruby rages.

She flies out of her chair so fast that it crashes to the floor and tries to go over the table, her teeth barred and her arms out to grab the general. I grab her by her waist, trying to hold her back, but she fights like a feral animal. I manage to get her off the table and on her feet, but she's still struggling against me.

"Ruby!" I snap, trying to get her attention. Her shoulders heave and her body shakes with fury. I forcefully turn her to face me and hold her head so she has to look at me. "You need to calm down."

"Don't tell me to fucking cal—"

The door bangs open and Danny rushes in, coming to a halt when he sees that everything is under control... barely. "Everything okay in here?"

I don't look at Danny but instead, keep my eyes locked on my woman. "Ruby, is everything okay?"

She crosses her arms over her chest and huffs out a breath. "I'm not going to kill him if that's what you're asking."

"Good enough for me," Danny retorts and leaves the room, pulling the door shut behind him.

When I'm satisfied that Ruby is calm enough to return to the meeting, I right her chair and urge her to sit. I take my own seat and that's when I notice that Larry seems completely unaffected by her outburst. He hasn't moved a muscle. Come to think of it, he didn't so much as flinch when she launched herself in his direction.

"Miss Banks," he begins. "I know you're angry, and rightfully so, but I want you to know that I am very sorry for whatever harm I helped to bring you." When Ruby opens her mouth to speak, he holds up his hand. "Please, let me finish." He takes several deep breaths before continuing. "I know that 'sorry' doesn't fix it. It doesn't lessen your pain or suffering. It doesn't even begin to make up for anything Jensen or I did. But an apology is all I've got. An apology and this." He waves his hand to indicate the files.

"You're right, an apology does nothing to make me feel better," Ruby snaps. "Let's just go over the information so you can get the hell out of here. I don't want to be in your presence longer than I have to be."

"Can you start at the beginning and go through each *incident* in detail?" Isaiah asks. "Documentation is great, but I'd also like to hear everything from you."

"Of course."

The next four and a half hours is spent doing exactly that. Larry goes through the files, page by page, explaining what they are and answering all of our questions. The process is draining, both physically and emotionally. Larry packs up his copies of the files, along with the laptop he brought. When he stands to leave, he seems lighter, less burdened.

"I have one more piece of information to give you."

"Jesus, there's more?" I growl.

"Jensen will be back in Texas tomorrow. He called this morning and demanded that I make myself available to him."

Larry pulls out a slip of paper from his pocket and sets it on the table. "Here's the time and location of that meeting."

Without another word, he walks out of the room, briefcase in hand. Isaiah reaches across the table and picks up the paper, unfolding it to read the information.

"Ten o'clock in the morning at this address." He turns the note for me to read.

"Isn't that Jensen's home address?" I ask.

"Lemme see," Ruby demands and rips the paper from Isaiah's fingers. She shakes her head. "No. The numbers are the same, but the street name is different. It looks familiar though."

I pull out my cell phone and open an internet browser to run a quick search. "Looks like it's a storage place."

Isaiah grins. "Whatever it is, we'll be there."

29

RUBY

"Where the hell is he?"

The crackle of Isaiah's voice plays through the earpiece they gave me to wear. Liam and I are on one side of the building, while Isaiah and Danny are up on a hill on the other. We didn't want to bring too many club members, for fear that Jensen would realize something was up. The two vehicles we brought are parked out of sight in one of the empty storage units that somehow, Danny managed to secure for the afternoon.

"I don't know," Liam responds. "But I've got a bad feeling about this. He was supposed to be here twenty minutes ago."

"Do you still have eyes on Larry?" I ask.

"Affirmative. He's still in his vehicle, as instructed," Danny responds. "He's getting fidgety though."

"We give it another ten minutes and then we get out of here," Isaiah says, frustration making his tone gritty. "The detectives only agreed to give us this one shot and even that was pushing it. Danny's buddy wasn't too thrilled with the prospect."

Danny's chuckle rasps through the headset. "You ain't

kidding. He only agreed because we've helped them with a lot of cases over the years. And I promised we'd bring Jensen in alive. He owed me. I think I'm gonna owe him now though."

The headset goes quiet, and I lean against the building as we wait. I can't help but to keep glancing at my watch and with each tick of the second hand, my muscles tighten. Liam is hyper focused on the parking lot and surrounding area.

The crunch of tires over gravel draws our attention and I shift my position so the wall isn't in my line of sight.

"Black SUV pulling into the lot," Isaiah warns.

"We see it," Liam says.

We watch as the SUV turns into the parking space next to Larry's Lincoln Navigator. I hold my breath when I see the door open and a booted foot steps out. My body deflates when I see the black wavy hair at the top of the twenty-something year old guy that's attached to the booted foot. This isn't Jensen.

"False alarm," Liam remarks, his shoulders falling. "Dammit!"

"I hate to call it but he's obviously not coming," Isaiah says. "Let's get…"

I miss the rest of what he says because my burner phone vibrates against my leg and I focus on getting it out and answering the call. It's Larry.

"Where the fuck is he?" I demand.

"He just texted me the coordinates of a different location."

"What? Why?"

"Who knows? Probably because he's an ass and is having fun pulling the strings."

"Text him back and say you'll be there," I bark. "We'll be right behind you."

I end the call and turn to Liam, who's staring at me with raised brows. "Let's go. We've got another location."

"Ruby, we can't go chasing Jensen around Texas," Liam argues.

"Watch me!" I shout and turn to make my way to the lot.

Liam calls after me but I ignore him. I don't care if I'm being reckless. I don't care if Danny called in a favor and this will screw him over. I don't fucking care what happens as long as Jensen is in cuffs or dead when the dust settles.

"Ruby!" Isaiah barks as he skids to a halt in front of me. "What do you think you're doing?"

"I'm doing what you can't!"

I storm off down the row where the vehicles are. Footsteps echo behind me and it's clear that they belong to more than one person. The guys could easily stop me if they really wanted to. I'm not faster than they are. Hell, I'm not even running. Instead, they're staying back and giving me some space.

When I yank open the door that the first car is behind, the footsteps grow closer. A hand latches onto my arm when I reach out to open the driver's side door.

"Ruby, c'mon. This is ridiculous," Liam pleads.

I glare at his hand and then lift my eyes to his. "Let. Go."

His grip tightens. "No. I'm not letting you do—"

"Liam," Isaiah snaps.

Liam's attention is diverted long enough that I'm able to dislodge myself from his hold and get in the car. I can hear their raised voices as they argue but I can't make out their words. Not that I give a shit what they're saying. My sole focus is on following Larry and getting to Jensen.

I lower the visor and the key falls into my hand. The engine roars to life and when I ensure that I have a clear path out of the unit, I shift the car into drive and take off. When I glance in the rearview mirror, I see Liam and Isaiah jump into the second vehicle. Danny must have gotten it while I was making my getaway.

I turn left out of the lot and see Larry's car up ahead. I stomp on the accelerator until I'm right behind him and then back off a bit so it's not obvious I'm following him. Larry knows I'm behind him, but I don't want someone else to catch on.

We drive through a few residential neighborhoods, through the city, and circle back toward the storage units. I have no idea where we're going, and unease settles in my gut. What the hell is Jensen up to? Or is this Larry's doing?

Another look in the mirror and I'm happy to see that Liam, Isaiah, and Danny are still behind me, not too close but enough so that it relieves some of my worry. If something goes wrong, at least they'll know right away.

We pass the storage units again and Larry weaves his way into a more rural area, heading north. An hour passes and it's not long before we're the only three cars on the road. I grab my phone and hit speed dial for Larry.

"Where are we going?" I demand when he answers.

"I'm not sure," he replies, frustration tinging his voice. "He keeps sending me different coordinates. I'm just following them."

"Have you talked to him again or is it all through text?"

"Text."

I heave a sigh. "Okay. There has to be an end to his game eventually. And we'll play until he can't anymore."

I hang up and use my thumb to text Liam.

Coordinates keep changing. In this till the end.

I navigate a sharp curve and then glance at the incoming text.

Liam: Right behind you.

A smile tugs at my lips and I place the phone under my thigh on the seat. No doubt Liam is gonna read me the riot act when this is all over but he's still here, backing me up. The seat vibrates as another text comes through.

Liam: We WILL talk about this later.

I know we will.

As I continue to follow Larry, my mind races through the possibilities of where Jensen has him going. The one that concerns me the most is Gila National Forest, but I dismiss that option quickly because it's another hour or two away.

We wind through a few more curves and as I'm straightening out the wheel at the end of the last one, I see Larry's Lincoln fishtail and watch in horror as he fails to regain control and runs off the road, into a wooded area. He narrowly misses a few trees but ends up slamming into one, head on, a few hundred yards in.

I stomp on the brake and pull over, bringing the car to a stop and throwing the door open. I take off running, intent on getting to Larry and getting him away from the wreckage.

I pass the trees he missed and when I reach the rear bumper of the Lincoln, searing pain at the back of my skull registers.

As I'm falling, I'm dimly aware of leaves floating in my line of sight and the last thing I see before I black out is Jensen, standing over me holding a wooden baseball bat.

30

LIAM

"What the fucking hell just happened?"

Danny's voice sounds very far away despite the fact that he's in the driver's seat right next to me. I can't take my eyes off of Larry's Lincoln as it swerves uncontrollably and then launches off the road.

"Pull over!" I shout, panic rising as I see Ruby doing the same and then jumping out of her car to run toward the wreckage.

I throw my door open before our vehicle even comes to a stop.

"Ruby!" I scream.

She keeps running and when she winds through the trees, I lose sight of her. My legs burn as I navigate the path she took, my eyes never straying away from my target: Larry's SUV.

Leaves crunch behind me and I glance over my shoulder to see Danny and Isaiah. We're all three running as hard and as fast as we can. When I reach the wreckage, I don't see Ruby. Danny whizzes by me to check on Larry but my focus remains on finding Ruby.

I spin in circles, searching, screaming her name, silently begging for her to respond. She doesn't.

"Look at this."

I stop turning and look at the spot on the ground where Isaiah is crouched. I squat next to him and run my fingers over the leaves. When I lift my hands back up, they're sticky with a crimson substance. My stomach bottoms out.

"Larry's dead."

Isaiah and I lift our heads and stare at Danny. He's scrolling through a phone and when his eyes widen, we both stand to see what he's looking at. It's a text that Larry received two minutes before he lost control and when I read the words, my heart skips a beat.

Just a bit farther.

"Goddammit!" My fist bounces off the fender of the Lincoln and I barely register the pain that spreads through my hands. "This wasn't an accident."

"You're gonna want to see this," Danny says as he turns and walks back to the driver's side window. He points at Larry's slumped body and asks, "See that?"

"Is that—"

"A bullet hole?" Danny nods as he speaks. "Sure is."

"He was lying in wait." Isaiah squints as he looks in all directions. "That's from a sniper rifle."

"Jensen isn't a sniper," I argue, needing him to be wrong. Needing my gut to be wrong. Fucking needing Ruby to pop out from behind a tree and yell 'gotcha'.

"Not as a profession, no," Isaiah agrees. "Doesn't mean he doesn't have the skill."

"Let's fan out and see what we can find. There's no way Jenson got Ruby to go willingly, and we were right behind her. They're not far."

We separate and it isn't a minute later I hear a whistle pierce the air. I recognize it as Isaiah's, and I take off toward him. When I see him crouched next to a sniper setup, my worst fears start clawing their way past all of the adrenaline that should be getting me through this.

"That was a lot of blood back by the car," I recall. "You don't think he...?

I can't even voice the question out loud so it's good that Isaiah knows me so well.

"No. He didn't shoot her." He checks out the sniper rifle and points to something. "Only one bullet has been discharged. The rest of the clip is full."

"Then where the hell are they and what did he do to her?"

Isaiah stands and steps up to me, toe to toe. He rests his hands on my shoulders, trying to ground me.

"I don't know, brother. But she's not dead."

"You don't know that," I snap.

"Yeah, he does." I turn toward Danny, who stops walking when he reaches us. "Think about it, man. He's not going to kill her."

"Are you fucking kidding me?" I explode, shoving away from Isaiah to pace. "He's already killed three people, maybe four if Stephanie is dead. You really think he'd hesitate to put a bullet in Ruby?"

"Yes, I do." The confidence in Isaiah's voice does little to convince me. "He clearly knew that Larry had met with us. He has no idea what information Larry passed on. He needs to keep Ruby alive so he can find that out. He's not going to kill her until he's sure he's covered all of his bases where Larry is concerned. And so far, he has no fucking clue what those bases are."

What he says makes sense, but it doesn't calm me down. How long before he breaks Ruby? Before he gets the information they think he wants? How hurt is she already? Can she fight back? Where the fuck did he take her?

So many questions and zero answers.

"Danny, call your detective buddy," I demand. "You're gonna need to call in another favor."

"Man, I don't have any more favors to call in."

"I don't fucking care," I growl as I haul him up onto his toes by his jacket. "We need more eyes on this area and a police helicopter is the fastest way to accomplish that. Make it happen."

I shove him away from me and turn back to Isaiah. "I'm going to search. You can either come with me or wait here while he sorts this shit out with his buddy."

I take off and head deeper into the woods. My mind races, my lungs burn… my heart hurts. Isaiah keeps up with me and while we don't speak, it's comforting somehow to have him by my side. I don't know what I'll do if we can't find Ruby, or worse, find her dead. I'm going to need him if that happens.

"Ruby!" I shout her name, over and over, until I'm hoarse and can't shout one more time.

I'm coming, Ruby love. Just hold on a little longer.

Ruby

My eyes flutter open and I squeeze them shut again to ward off the agony. It doesn't work. I feel like I'm laying over a boulder and that boulder is bouncing. I force my eyes open into a squint and see leaves and sticks and what appears to be the forest floor passing beneath me.

What the fuck hap—

All at once, the memory floods into my brain. The storage

unit, following Larry, Larry crashing, me running. And then I remember Jensen's eyes, the baseball bat.

As everything hits me, I register that I'm being carried like a sack of flour over a shoulder. I try to raise myself up but am unsuccessful. My body feels sluggish, my limbs heavy. Did he drug me?

"Hello, Ruby."

At the sound of Jensen's voice, a spike in my adrenaline wars with whatever he pumped into me and I'm able to move a little easier. I lash out, pounding his back with my fists, kicking my legs as hard as I can. I flail around, doing anything and everything I can to get him to drop me.

He flips me over his shoulder onto the ground and the wind is knocked out of me. "You always were the most difficult."

As I try to catch my breath, he reaches into his jacket pocket and pulls out a syringe. I make a grab for it and miss, giving him the opportunity he needs to jab it into my thigh. Moments later, I fade into a black abyss.

When my eyes flutter open, I quickly register that I'm lying on my back. I don't hear the sounds I'd expect to hear in the woods. No crunching leaves, no bugs or animals scurrying about. Nothing. And I can't see anything because I'm surrounded by pitch black.

Bile rises up my throat and I roll over in time to puke the contents of my stomach onto the floor. *Floor?* When the heaving subsides, I roll to my other side and run my hands over the surface I'm on. It's smooth, like polished granite, but that makes no sense.

It takes me three tries before I'm able to sit up. I swivel my head and reach out my arms to feel for anything that can tell me where I'm at. At the very moment my hand comes into contact with what I think is a wall, a light flips on and is blindingly bright.

I yank my arm back to cover my eyes but the footsteps I hear coming closer force me to drop it so I can see.

"That dose lasted much longer."

Jensen grabs a chair and drags it next to me. He sits and crosses a booted foot over his knee.

"Where are we?" I ask, my voice clearer than I was expecting.

"Oh, this?" He lifts his hands and twists back and forth indicating the four walls around us. "You like it? The company that built it promised it would help me survive anything." He chuckles. "Doomsday prepping, I think they called it. This particular design is their 'Zombie Apocalypse' model." He casually leans back in the chair. "But I call it my insurance plan."

"Insurance for what?"

He lunges forward and wraps his fingers around my throat, squeezing until spots dance in front of me. "Against you, you stupid cunt." Spittle flies from his mouth and hits my cheek.

He pushes me, causing me to fall back onto my ass.

"So, you are afraid of me?" I taunt.

I know I shouldn't, but I can't stop myself. He stands so quickly, I don't see it coming. His foot lands in the middle of my chest, pinning me to the ground. He bends as far as he can and sneers in my face.

"There is nothing scary about you," he says through clenched teeth. "Now Larry, on the other hand, he scared me." Jensen shrugs. "He knew too much. Fortunately, he can't hurt me anymore. And as soon as I know what he told you, I'll show you how *not* scared of you I am."

I grab his ankle and, turning my body, yank his foot out from under him. He slams into the floor with a grunt, and I manage to get to my knees.

"Maybe you should be."

I brace my hands on my legs to leverage myself up. Jensen reaches out and his fingers latch onto the laces of my shoes. He's not able to knock me off balance but he is able to stop me from getting the fuck away from him.

With my foot locked in his grasp, I kick my leg to shake him off, but he's too strong. And the blow to my head, mixed with the drugs, means I'm weak and unable to fight like I need to.

Fuck that!

I change tactics, realizing that I won't win a physical fight. But maybe I stand a chance if I can beat him in a mental game.

"Let me ask you something," I begin and then add, "Sir."

Jensen maintains his hold on me and nods.

"Do you really think I was stupid enough to meet with Larry, follow him all this way, without some insurance of my own?"

His eyes widen and that's when I know I've got him. He's so egotistical and sure of himself that he really believed I wouldn't have a backup plan.

"That's what I thought." I glance pointedly at where he's touching me. "I suggest you let me go, Jensen. I'm not the kinda girl that no one is going to miss. You will be hunted if anything happens to me. And the people that will hunt you?" I shake my head and make a tsking sound. "You don't want to go up against them. You won't survive."

His hollow laugh echoes in the space. "A bunch of washed-up veterans who straddle Harleys because they're compensating for a lack of something else in their lives? Yeah, I think I'll take my chances."

"And I can't even look you in the eye and tell you, honestly, that you'll live to regret it." I pause and tilt my head. "Wanna know why?" The question is rhetorical so I don't bother giving him a chance to respond. "Because you'll be dead."

He throws his head back and laughs and when he does, his grip loosens. In this moment, I feel like a movie-goer in a packed theater of the latest horror flick release. My brain screams 'for the love of God, don't run toward the danger' but my body has other plans. Just like that teenage chick in the movie who's running into the dark garage full of sharp tools and blunt objects, I edge closer to the danger.

"How?" I ask, leaning over *him* now with my foot on *his* chest. "How did you figure it out that Larry came to me? How did you do all of this?"

"Larry isn't the only connection I have." When I arch my brow in question, he explains. "I've always had a backup plan. I may have been paying Larry well but eventually, I knew he'd retire and would no longer be able to serve my needs. When he told me he was out, I called in my… reinforcements."

"So the moment he called me, you knew?"

"Ah, give her a gold star," he mocks. From there it was pretty easy. I made sure that, even as he was turning on me, I was still pulling the strings."

This man is diabolical. He has every single person around him fooled and the ones he can't fool? He manipulates them until they do what he wants. As evil as I knew him to be, the reality is, he's so much worse.

"What's your plan?"

"My plan?" he counters.

"Yeah. When you're done with me, what's next?"

He stares at me like I've lost my mind. Who knows? Maybe I have. I'm standing here, pinning him down, and making conversation. I should be knocking his ass out and running. But there are some *things* I have to know.

"Back to work, I suppose."

"You're delusional."

"I think you mean brilliant."

"Why me?" I ask as if he hadn't spoken.

"Why you what?"

"What was it about me that made you think I was an easy target?"

He shrugs. "The glint in your eye on the day you met me. You were so in love with the idea of the Army. A girl and her dreams." He pauses to let that sink in and then gets serious. "You're all alike. You come into the Army thinking you're the same as us, thinking you can do whatever it is we do and so goddamned determined to prove it. Women like you? You never talk."

It's a sucker punch in the gut to realize he's right. Not about women not being equal. No, I firmly believe *we* can do anything a man can do in the military, or anywhere else for that matter. But when it comes to surviving and wanting to make it in a man's world, we're conditioned to keep our heads down and our mouths shut. We're all told to 'prove them wrong'. And that's exactly what I wanted to do.

Unable to stand him a second longer, I thrust a kick to the side of his head. The sound it makes hitting the floor is both sickening and rewarding. I waste no time in trying to escape because he's not knocked out, only stunned.

I reach the door to the bunker and am shocked to find a key hanging on the wall next to it. I yank it off the hook and shove it in the lock, pushing the door open when I hear it disengage.

He really is too sure of himself.

I race up the steps outside the door and come to a wooden hatch that appears flimsy. I push it up and it falls open, allowing me to climb my way free.

"Get the fuck back here!"

As I weave my way through the trees, stumbling over dead limbs as I go, Jensen remains close. Too close.

"You don't know your way around these woods like I do!" he shouts.

I keep bobbing and weaving, bobbing and weaving, praying like hell that I lose him. My lungs burn from exertion but I push through it, knowing that if I stop, I'm dead.

"Ruby!"

Jensen is closing in, so I run faster, harder.

"Ruby!"

Wait, that's not Jensen. I know that voice. Even as I run, I strain to see if I hear it again.

"Ruuuuubyyyy!"

I was right.

"Liam!" I shout into the night. "Liam, where are you?!"

I stop at the closest tree and flatten my back against it. Liam will never find me if I keep running. I don't want Jensen to catch me but it's a chance I have to take. I look around me to see if there's anything I can call out about my location that will assist Liam but not tip off Jensen. Multiple sets of footsteps sound as if they're getting closer. Is it Jensen? Liam and the guys? All of them? I look to my right and spot the hatch that I climbed out of. I didn't realize that I'd run in circles, but it doesn't matter. Seeing it gives me an idea.

"Lock the door, Liam," I shout into the wind. "Lock the fucking door!"

My hope is that the sound of my voice will give him some idea of where I am in relation to him but also that he realizes I'm telling him to look for some sort of door.

"Didn't make it far, now did you?"

I whip my head to the left and see Jensen standing about ten feet away, a gun trained on me.

"He'll kill you," I say, loudly in the hopes that Liam will hear us talking. "You kill me, he kills you."

Jensen shrugs. "Not if I kill you both first."

That's true but what Jensen doesn't know is that Liam isn't alone. And if he does know that, then he definitely has a death wish.

"Drop the gun."

My gaze shifts and I see Liam, standing next to Jensen, his weapon pointing at Jensen's head.

"I said," Liam growls. "Drop. The. Fucking. Gun."

Jensen glances over his shoulder toward Liam. "I don't think so."

"Fuck, you're stupid."

I look on the other side of Jensen and see Isaiah standing there, shaking his head as if he were watching a child do something silly and getting a kick out of it.

Time seems to stand still, all three men ready and willing to take a human life if necessary. Jensen looks at me and I can see the moment he makes up his mind that he doesn't care if he dies out here in these woods.

As I watch Jensen's finger begin to move, Danny appears out of nowhere. Two things happen simultaneously: Jensen pulls the trigger and Danny hits Jensen over the head with the butt of his weapon, dropping him in a heap on the ground.

A burning sensation tears through my body and as it registers that I've been shot, I collapse.

This time, the pain is so intense, I welcome the darkness.

31

LIAM

I hate hospitals.

With good reason. Brotherhood members have spent way too much time within four walls that look just like these. I pace the length of the ER waiting room, impatient for an update from the surgeon.

"She's in good hands." Danny slaps me on the back when he approaches. "The doctors in this hospital are top notch. Trust me, we've used them a lot."

I shove my hands through my hair. "How long does it take to remove a fucking bullet? Cut her open, pluck the bullet out, close her up. That shouldn't take this long. What if something went wrong? What if she's dead and they're trying to figure out how to te—"

"Brother," Isaiah interrupts. "Stop. She will be fine, I promise. Like the surgeon told you before they took her in, the bullet didn't hit anything vital."

"It lodged into her spleen!" I argue.

"Which can be removed." Isaiah rests a hand on my shoulder. "Why don't we go to the cafeteria and get some coffee?"

"I'm not going anywhere." I step away from him and plop

down in a chair, resting my head in my hands. "Shit, Isaiah, when I saw her go down after getting shot? I thought that was it. She was done. And then I heard the helicopter and that gave me some hope, ya know?"

"I know. I'm glad the detective had a medical helicopter on standby in case we found her. No telling how long we'd have had to wait for one to arrive if they had to come any farther."

"They loaded her up and by then, she was conscious, coherent." Isaiah nods as he listens but doesn't interrupt. "And then... I lost count of the number of times she faded in and out. She coded once and again, I thought her number had been called. But somehow, we made it here and her heart was still beating. What if the next time I see her, it's not?"

"It will be," he insists.

"And if it's not?" I repeat, brokenly. "I can't live without her. I don't want to live without her. Ruby is... man, she's the light to my dark. She makes everything shitty in the world a little more tolerable just because she's in it."

"And when she wakes up, you're gonna tell her that."

I sit up straight and twist in my chair so I can look Isaiah in the eyes. "You have to promise me something."

"Anything, brother. You know that."

"Promise me that, if she doesn't make it..." I swallow past the lump in my throat. "Promise me you won't leave my side. You'll keep me from the ledge I'll want to jump from. Can you do that? Can you promise to get me through it?"

"Liam Strong?"

I stand up and face the nurse who just called my name. Before I walk toward her, I look back at Isaiah. "Promise me."

"I promise."

I take a deep breath and go to the nurse, my heart in my throat.

"Are you Liam?"

"Yes."

"Miss Banks is asking for you."

Ruby

My head is foggy but now that I have morphine flowing through my IV, the pain is tolerable. I stare out the window while I wait for the nurse to bring Liam in. The sky is changing colors as the sun rises, bringing with it a brand new day.

The door to my room creaks as it opens and I turn my head slowly, hoping it's Liam. My breath catches when I see him and when he tentatively starts walking toward me, as if he's afraid I'll fade away if he goes too fast, tears spring to my eyes.

Liam stops next to the bed and stares. I wait for him to reach out, to say something, anything. When he doesn't, I frown.

"What's wrong?"

The grin that spreads across his face is the best thing I've seen in what feels like forever. "I was afraid I'd never hear your voice again," he says, quietly, reverently.

"You know me better than that. I'm too much of a control freak to let someone else dictate when it's my time to die."

Liam throws his head back and laughs. When he regains his composure, he picks up my hand and kisses my knuckles. Then he gets serious.

"Ruby love, if you ever pull a stunt like that again…"

I smile at him when he can't finish his sentence. Liam is a fierce protector, a strong man who's not afraid to get his hands dirty. But when it comes to me, to the woman he loves, he's a softy.

"I'm sorry I scared you." I can't promise I'll never do something reckless again so I don't even bother lying.

Dismissing this line of conversation, whether because he knows I'm lying or he just doesn't want to talk about it, Liam changes the subject.

"What did the surgeon say? Everything went well?"

"I think so. I'm still a little muddy-headed from the anesthesia but I remember him saying they removed my spleen. They stitched up the gash at the back of my head but, lucky for me, it was right at the base of my skull at the edge of my hairline so they didn't have to shave any."

Liam chuckles. "That's good. Any idea when you'll get out of here?"

"A day or two, I think." A thought occurs to me. "Shit, do you and Isaiah need to get back to the club? I'm sure Danny or one of the ladies here will help me out until I can leave."

I don't want him to leave me of course, but I also don't want to be the reason that he abandons his family, even if for only a few days.

"I'm staying. Isaiah already called everyone and he's staying, too." I release the breath I didn't realize I was holding. "We've got a few things to wrap up here in Texas anyway." He rubs the back of his neck and looks away for a moment as if to collect his thoughts. "Jensen is still alive."

"Okay," I say, figuring that was the case. I remember Danny knocking him out and as full of rage as Liam was, I know he wouldn't kill a man if he didn't have to. "He's in custody though, right?"

Liam nods. "The police are handing him over to the military. He'll be court-martialed." He takes a deep breath. "You're still going to have to testify at a trial."

As recent as a few weeks ago, the thought of testifying would have sent me running. Now? Now I want to face the bastard and make sure that no stone is left unturned when it comes to what he's punished for.

"I'm good with that."

"I spoke with Eileen. She said the same thing."

"Good." A thought occurs to me. "What about Stephanie?"

"You don't know?"

I shake my head. "Know what?"

"She was in that bunker. There was another room where Jensen kept a bunch of supplies. She was tied up, barely breathing and unconscious, but alive."

"Oh thank God."

"She's in the ICU but expected to pull through. She's gonna have a long road ahead of her as far as dealing with the trauma but we've already spoken to the president of the Seattle chapter and they're going to stick close and help her through it. He's sending one of his guys down here to be with her before she's released so that there's at least one person who isn't a stranger."

"Wow. That's..."

"That's family, Ruby love. Our family."

The mention of family has me thinking of my parents and my emotions whip around like a flag in the wind. I miss my parents. I did what I had to in order to protect them, but I don't have to keep my distance anymore. I can call them. I can see them. I can hug them.

"I already called them."

I lift my eyes at Liam's words. "You did?"

"Of course I did. You're their daughter and you were hurt. They needed to know."

Tears spill down my cheeks. "Thank you," I whisper.

"They'll be here tomorrow. The earliest flight they could book is a red-eye and Danny is going to pick them up at the airport and bring them here. Should be here around seven in the morning or so."

"I can't believe you did that for me."

"And I'd do it a million more times if it makes you happy."

"I love you so much, Liam."

He gently lifts my arm and stretches out next to me on the hospital bed, tucking my hand in the crook of his elbow.

"I love you too, Ruby love."

EPILOGUE

RUBY

Six months later...

"It is the finding of this panel that you, Douglas Jensen, are guilty of one count of murder in the second degree, two counts of murder in the first degree, two counts of attempted murder in the first degree, false imprisonment, thirty-six counts of rape, two charges of kidnapping, and conduct unbecoming of an Army Captain."

My jaw drops and I seek out Liam's hand. He laces his fingers through mine and squeezes, assuring me that he's right here, beside me like he said he would be. Arms come around me from behind in a hug and I hear my mom's voice in my ear.

"You did it, honey," she whispers through her tears. "You burned his world to the ground."

I lean forward to look around Liam and see Eileen sitting there, tears streaming down her face. Stephanie, along with the Brotherhood member that's been glued to her side since she was released from the hospital, are on the other side of Eileen. All I can think is, no, *we* did it. Sure, we didn't take on the entire military and their policies like we were determined to do but maybe we can work on that now that Jensen is no longer a threat.

There's so much noise going on around me that I almost miss the clank of the gavel. I look up and see the presiding military judge waiting to issue sentencing.

"Douglas Jensen, normally at this phase of a military trial, I issue a sentence and go home. But nothing about this trial has been normal. You, sir, are a disgrace to the uniform. Not only do you deserve the maximum punishment I can give, but I also firmly believe there's a special place in Hell with your name on it. That being said, I think you're going to get there a lot more quickly than you'd hoped." The judge pauses and lifts a piece of paper to read from. "Douglas Jensen, you are hereby stripped of your title as Army Captain and any commendations you have received. Any monetary benefits that you were entitled to are revoked. Furthermore, I impose the maximum sentence allowable under military law and sentence you to death by lethal injection." He bangs the gavel. "Court is adjourned."

Liam jumps up and lifts me into his arms to spin me around. I can't stop the tears from falling or the laughter that's mixed with them. It's over. It's finally over and Jensen got every bit of the punishment he deserves.

Not all of his victims were willing to come in and testify and surprisingly, the military respected that. They requested written statements from those not willing to come and every single living victim complied with that request.

As hard of a decision as it was, we all agreed to keep Larry's name out of any of our statements. That doesn't mean I, or anyone, condone what he did, but he already paid with his life. And the decision to hold up our end of the deal was more for his wife than him.

When Liam sets me back on my feet, I can't stop from

rising on my tiptoes and peaking around me to the other side of the room. Jane, Jensen's wife, is sitting alone, quietly sobbing into a tissue. My heart hurts for her. With each new piece of evidence introduced during the trial, I think she died a little inside because she genuinely seemed shocked. Fortunately, she has family in Italy and can get out of Texas and away from assholes who will hound her about her husband's actions for the rest of her life.

"You ready?" Liam whispers in my ear, pulling my attention back to him.

"For what?"

"To go home."

"More than ready."

He takes my hand and leads me outside. When the sun hits my face, I pause and look at the sky, grateful that I'm still alive to enjoy it. We walk as a group to the Harleys we arrived on, and before I can throw my leg over the seat, Liam drops to one knee.

A hush falls over the large group of spectators and Liam grins at me.

"I was going to wait until we got home but this feels like the right time." He reaches into his pocket and pulls out a black velvet box. When he lifts the lid, a sparkly diamond winks at me. "Ruby, I've loved you for what feels like a lifetime. I can't promise you that life with me will always be smooth sailing. What I can promise, is I'll love you through any storm, I'll stand by you always and protect you fiercely. I will treat you as my equal, the other half of my soul. Will you marry me?"

I launch myself into his arms, knocking him back on the pavement, and cover his face in kisses. "Yes. Yes, yes, yes."

"Finally," Isaiah says from behind me.

Liam and I shift so we can look at him and he reaches

into his back pocket and pulls out his wallet. He flips that open and brings out a folded up, tattered envelope.

"Here," he thrusts it in our direction. "This is for you."

I grab the envelope before Liam does and when I unfold it, my heart skips a beat. I feel Liam's eyes on me, waiting for me to say something, anything.

"What is it?" he asks impatiently.

I scoot closer and hold it out so he can read it too.

Give this to Ruby and Liam. You'll know when the time is right.

Liam looks up from the shakily scrawled words and right at Isaiah. "Dusty?" When Isaiah nods, Liam asks, "When?"

"I got it in the mail a few days after his death. I had no fucking clue what it meant but figured he had a good reason for sending it to me. I put it in a drawer and when you finally opened up about Ruby, I moved it to my wallet so I always had it on me, just in case." He laughs. "I just hope this is the right time."

I open the envelope and pull out the lined paper. Together, Liam and I read the words.

If you're reading this, then you've finally realized I knew what I was talking about. May the two of you always remember that you have each other and never have to walk through this life alone. I love you both and wish I could be at the wedding, but I know you'll have a toast, just for me. And none of the cheap shit either.

Love,

Uncle Dusty

P.S. I wouldn't mind having a kid named after me (wink, wink).

SNEAK PEEK AT BROKEN LOYALTY

BOOK FOUR IN THE BROKEN REBEL BROTHERHOOD: NEXT GENERATION SERIES

Finn…

Wounded Warrior, that's what they call me. But that's not who I am. I'm broken, physically and mentally, beyond repair. And I'm no warrior. The only thing I'm good for is sharing my story when the mood strikes me and ignoring the pitying looks when storytime is over.

Why, then, can't I ignore the searing stare of the blonde beauty? I try but she is a perfect representation of my old life, my pre-war life. A life I took for granted. Even worse, she keeps dangling a very tempting carrot in front of me and tearing down walls that I carefully built to protect myself.

Isabelle…

It's not easy being the twin of an MC president but it's a position I've accepted and learned to embrace. I grew up knowing that our club would always be my home, my North Star in a demented world. I never dreamed I would find another place, another family that would give me even more purpose in life. Working with veterans feeds my soul in ways the club can't.

Then he shows up and rocks my foundation. He's the

very best of both worlds, but he doesn't see it. Within minutes of first laying eyes on him, I vow to do whatever it takes to help him figure out how to bridge the divide. There's a giant flaw in my plan though. I'm the one who ends up needing him. I'm the one who may not survive without his help. And I'm not entirely certain he's capable of giving it.

PROLOGUE

FINN

"Would anyone else like to share?"

I let my gaze wander over the faces of others like me. Their expressions range from those of denial to anger to bargaining to depression to acceptance. The five stages of grief all on display in one cramped room.

"Finn, we haven't heard from you in a while." Chris the leader of the group hones in on me. They always do. "How about you share your story, give some hope to any newcomers here today."

Hope my fucking ass. There is no hope. There's nothing but endless pain and suffering. But that's not what Chris wants me to say. That's not what these people need to hear. I may be firmly rooted in the anger stage with no chance in hell of moving past it, but that doesn't have to be their fate.

I press my fist into my thigh and massage my way down to my knee, or what used to be my knee. Thanks to a bomb, it's a titanium albatross that I'll never rid myself of.

I don't say any of that though. Wounded Warriors is my last link to a world I'm no longer a part of and I refuse to do or say anything that could jeopardize it. So, I bite my tongue and force the words that everyone wants to hear past my lips.

"I'm glad you all made the decision to come to group. I think you'll find that, the more you attend, the faster you can accept your injury and the changes that come along with it." To my own ears, the lie is obvious. Based on the intense looks from everyone else, they don't have a fucking clue. "It's been one year, four months, two weeks and three days since I lost my leg, but who's counting?" I chuckle, like I always do at this point, and then lift my pant leg to reveal my above the knee amputation. "Sure, at first, I wished I had died in the bombing. I begged and pleaded with every single doctor and nurse that came near me to finish the job the bomb couldn't. But they never gave up on me." I pause for dramatic affect. "And eventually, *I* didn't want to give up on me."

There are hushed whispers, looks of disbelief, and smiles of encouragement. The reactions are the same no matter what.

"I strongly encourage each of you to find a buddy. Talk to those in attendance at these groups, learn their story, their struggle, and be each other's cheerleader. You aren't alone. I know it feels like it. I know that you all feel as if you're the only person in the world who's going through it, like no one else could possibly understand. But that's not true. You are not alone."

The moment I finish speaking, Chris stands and walks over to me. He thrusts out a hand and I shake it. It's his thing. I don't get it. Hell, I don't even like it. But if it makes him feel better, I can suck it up.

"Well, that was certainly a message we all need to hear sometimes," Chris says. His face falls when there isn't an immediate response from the others but he quickly recovers. "Now, as I told you last month, I am transferring to another state and will no longer be running these groups. But, my replacement is amazing and I know you'll love her."

Her?

Chris glances at the clock on the wall. "She should have been here by now and I hate to end it before she arrives. Does anyone else have anything they'd like to share? Any issues you'd like to discuss?"

"Yeah," the guy sitting in the third chair to my right. "What do you know about this new person?"

That's a valid question but really? What does it matter what Chris knows? She's either got what it takes to inspire broken vets to not get wrapped up in self-pity parties or she doesn't. And quite frankly, if she's not a vet herself, I doubt she'll have what it takes.

"Her name is Isabelle Mallory," Chris begins. "I don't know much about her other than her experience is vast when it comes to trauma and she's excited to take on her new position."

"Perfect," another guy grumbles. "She's as broken as the rest of us."

"No, that's not what I said," Chris replies with a frown on her face. "Her trauma experience is from a professional standpoint, not personal."

And there it is, the proof that I'm right. She isn't going to be cut out for this. No way in hell she's going to know what to do if she's not experienced a traumatic event herself.

"Well," Chris glances at the clock again. "I hate to keep you any longer so feel free to leave if you want. I'll stick around for anyone who wants to wait on Miss Mallory."

The room empties out quickly but I'm hesitant to leave. Chris is a good dude. A little too upbeat and positive for my taste but he actually gives a damn about his clients.

"Why don't you call her?" I suggest. "Maybe she got stuck in traffic or something."

Chris pulls out his phone and turns it on. Funny, I think he's the only one that actually turns his phone off like the sign on the door says. When it's powered up, I watch as his fingers fly over the screen.

He holds the phone up. "Hopefully she responds." His cell dings and after reading the text, his shoulders sag. "It seems she got stuck in traffic. She's still on her way but likely an hour out."

"Shit," I say because it seems like something I should be upset about.

"I'm just gonna text her back and tell her to turn around. I have dinner reservations with my wife and she'd kill me if I cancel again."

Against my better judgement, and again, because I like the guy, I offer an alternative. "I can stay."

"Are you sure?"

He looks so hopeful that no matter how much I want to revoke the offer, I don't. I even throw in another lie to sound happy about it.

"Sure. It's no problem. I don't have any other plans tonight." Other than a six pack of beer and taking my frustration out of my punching bag.

Chris stands and puts his jacket on. Next, he throws his messenger bag—a fucking messenger bag—over his head so it hangs across his body. What the actual fuck?

"Thank you, Finn." He sticks out his hand. He's seriously going to make me shake it, one last time. And I do, because it's *one last time*. "It's been a pleasure working with you. I'm proud of the progress you've made."

"Thanks," I mumble, uncomfortable with the praise.

He walks toward the door but before he leaves, he looks back over his shoulder. "Hey Finn?"

"Yeah?"

"Give her a chance, will ya? She just might surprise you."

That's the moment I realize that Chris isn't as dumb as he looks and I'm not as good a liar as I think I am. I can't help but laugh.

"Fine. I'll give her a chance."

Two hours later, Isabelle Mallory still hasn't shown her face. Well, she blew her chance. I turn off the lights and make my way outside to the parking lot. As I step off the curb, heading in the direction of my Harley, another bike whizzes by me, narrowly missing my damn toes.

"Hey asshole!" I shout. "Watch where the fuck you're going."

I keep walking and see that 'asshole' is now parked in the spot next to mine. I take in the Harley, with his matte black and chrome finishes and hate that I'm envious. It's a damn nice bike. Clearly custom and tailored to its owner.

Speaking of its owner, they throw their leg over the bike and when the helmet is removed, my jaw drops. Standing in skintight jeans and a black leather jacket is a woman. And not just any woman. She's a dead-ringer for the woman I always envisioned on my arm through life... before I was blown to hell by a bomb and one leg short.

She shakes her head and finger combs her long blonde hair. Seemingly satisfied that she's fixed her helmet hair, she whirls around and runs straight into my chest, practically bouncing back at the contact.

"Fuck, I'm sorry."

Not what I would have expected to come out of that sinfully sexy mouth.

"God, you must think I'm an idiot. I didn't mean to cut it so close back there." She hitches a thumb over her shoulder to indicate where she almost mowed me down. "It's just...I'm running very late and traffic was a bitch and then I had the address wrong so that de—"

She slams her mouth shut and breathes deeply through

her nose. This does nothing to cool the boner that's forming in my boxer briefs. It's the first time my dick has reacted to anything since the bombing so I'm not even mad that I might embarrass myself.

"Let me start over." She smiles and even under the flickering light that supposedly makes the parking lot 'safer', there's no denying the way it reaches her eyes. "Hi."

She thrusts her hand out for me to shake and without thinking, I take it.

"I'm Isabelle Mallory."

Son of a fucking bitch.

ABOUT THE AUTHOR

Andi Rhodes is an author whose passion is creating romance from chaos in all her books! She writes MC (motorcycle club) romance with a generous helping of suspense and doesn't shy away from the more difficult topics. Her books can be triggering for some so consider yourself warned. Andi also ensures each book ends with the couple getting their HEA! Most importantly, Andi is living her real life HEA with her husband and their boxers.

For access to release info, updates, and exclusive content, be sure to sign up for Andi's newsletter at andirhodes.com.

ALSO BY ANDI RHODES

Broken Rebel Brotherhood

Broken Souls

Broken Innocence

Broken Boundaries

Broken Rebel Brotherhood: Complete Series Box set

Broken Rebel Brotherhood: Next Generation

Broken Hearts

Broken Wings

Broken Mind

Bastards and Badges

Stark Revenge

Slade's Fall

Jett's Guard

Soulless Kings MC

Fender

Joker

Piston

Greaser

Riker

Trainwreck

Squirrel

Gibson

Satan's Legacy MC

Snow's Angel

Toga's Demons

Magic's Torment

Printed in Great Britain
by Amazon